THE 7 POETS AND THE TROUBLESOME TIME MACHINE

By Ez Schwartz
and
Joe Schwartz
Illustrations by Kam Chan

Happy Happy Happy Publishing

To adventurers everywhere

This book is a work of fiction. Names, characters, places, and incidents are the product of the authors' imaginations or are used fictitiously. Any resemblance to actual events, locales, or persons, living or dead is entirely coincidental.

Copyright © 2014 by Ezra Schwartz and Joseph J. Schwartz

Illustrations copyright © 2014 by Kam Chan

All rights reserved. In accordance with the U.S. Copyright Act of 1976, the scanning, uploading, and electronic sharing of any part of this book without the permission of the publisher is unlawful piracy and theft of the author's intellectual property. If you would like to use material from the book (other than for review purposes), prior written permission must be obtained by contacting the publisher at permissions@happyhappyhappy.com.

Happy Happy Happy Publishing
P.O. Box 20078
New York, NY 10014

www.happyhappyhappy.com

The publisher is not responsible for websites or their content that are not owned by the publisher.

ISBN 978-0-9896575-1-8 (paperback)

First Edition: December 2014

Contents

1	The Troublesome Time Machine	1
2	The 7 Policemen	7
3	Grapecall	13
4	Rex	17
5	Agathon	23
6	Grapecalls	31
7	Blue	37
8	The Old Man	42
9	Yoder	50
10	The Man	58
11	Teodor	63
12	Frumbles	75
13	Bjarne	82
14	Fauntleroy	92
15	Ezra	103
16	The Chess Master	110
17	Egmont	120
	Epilogue	130

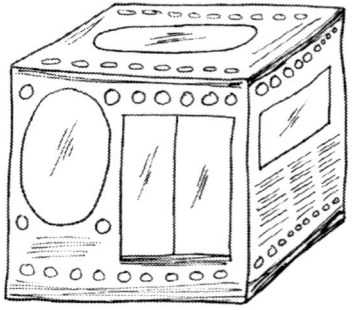

1
The Troublesome Time Machine

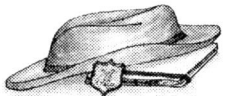

Everyone knew THAT house. It seemed every inch of it had something sticky smeared on it. Spaghetti sauce doorknobs, jelly-covered window sills, fudge-encrusted cabinets. No surface was safe from the sticky nine-year-old who lived inside. He had even managed to get melted gummy bears all over the roof shingles, although no one could ever figure out how in the world he got up there. His name was Grapecall and he never met anything slimy, greasy, pasty, or gooey that didn't seem to end up first on his hands and then, shortly thereafter, on some part of his home.

Fortunately for him, his dad didn't seem to

mind. While most parents would gently ask (or even yell or stomp their feet at) Grapecall to clean up his mess, Grapecall's dad was often too busy to even notice that his son had left a new stain or three. For Grapecall's dad was an inventor, always tinkering away at this gadget or that and lost in his dreams of the amazing contraptions he would bring to life.

In fact, Grapecall's dad had been lost in thought so often, and for so many years, that he had forgotten his own name. Evidently all the people in his neighborhood had forgotten his name as well. When asked about Grapecall's dad, they would simply say, "Oh, you mean the man who lives in the house with the door that's covered in melted marshmallow." Or "you must mean the man who's always bringing bags of strange electronic parts into his garage." So, after hearing people saying things like this for many years, Grapecall's dad would tell people who wanted to know his name that they could simply call him "The Man."

One day, while The Man was working on his latest invention, Grapecall was playing

with his ball. But because Grapecall's hands were covered with honey, each time he tried to throw the ball it remained stuck to his palm. As Grapecall scraped his hand against a desk lamp to detach the ball from his fingers, The Man turned to him and said, "Grape, why don't you wash that honey off your hands and the ball? I bet it bounces pretty high." Grapecall was so shocked that his dad noticed the mess he'd made that he immediately ran off to pry the bathroom door open (it was stuck to the doorframe with fruit rollups).

As soon as Grapecall had gone, The Man started working furiously. He ran inside his invention—a large box about the size of a very small bedroom—and placed an orange on top of a little square table. He exited the box, closing its door behind him, and went over to a wall covered with lights and buttons. He pushed a green button. The door to his invention slid open and two seconds later the top of the table popped up propelling the orange out of the door into The Man's hands. The man giggled. "Now to see if it works."

The Man quickly ran back inside his

invention, snapped the tabletop down, placed the orange back where it started, and, sliding the door behind him, ran back to the wall. "Fingers crossed," he murmured. He pushed a big blue button.

If you've ever seen a carousel going around and around at night with its lights making circular streaks in the air, the man's invention looked a lot like that. Except that as the lines of colored light surrounded the invention, it faded away and in thirty seconds had completely disappeared. The Man counted to three in his head, pushed the green button again, waited a bit more, and then pushed the big blue button one last time. Carousel lights. The small bedroom reappeared. But the door was open and the orange was nowhere to be seen.

"I DID IT! IT WORKS!"

"What works Dad?" asked Grapecall, now bouncing his very clean ball as he walked toward The Man.

"My time machine Grape! I sent an orange into the past!"

"Cool. Let me show you how high my ball

bounces." And Grapecall, not one drop of honey on his spotless hands, threw his ball as hard as he could at the floor. The ball bounced off the floor, careened into a picture of his Great-Aunt Peach Blossom, and bouncing off that, scored a direct hit on the big blue button.

"I'll get it," shouted Grapecall as he ran after the ball into what he thought was a small bedroom with lots of bright colored lights coming out of it.

The Man frantically ran to the button-covered wall. He pushed the stop button, but it was jammed with gum. He tried the emergency stop button, but it was stuck with ear wax. And before he could try something else the small bedroom was gone. *Just don't leave the time machine Grape,* he thought to himself, pressing the big blue button and praying that his son was alright. But when the colored lights dimmed and the time machine reappeared Grapecall was nowhere to be seen.

2
The 7 Policemen

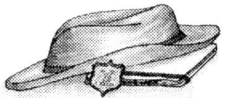

"I hate time travel. Always makes me want to throw up."

The other six policemen nodded. It had started to rain and the seven men stood silently across the street from The Man's home as the water collected on the brims of their fedoras and in puddles around their feet.

"Last time I couldn't eat for a week."

The wind started to pick up and a chill went through Yoder's body as he dug his hands into the pockets of his trench coat, wrapping it tightly around himself. He was done complaining.

"Maybe we could skip this one," said

Frumbles. "Someone else can look for the boy."

"There is no one else. That's why we're here." And with that Ezra started towards The Man's front door followed by Agathon, Fauntleroy, Bjarne, and Teodor.

"I've got the heebie jeebies," said Frumbles, nervously tapping his foot against the side of the curb.

Yoder looked at Frumbles, who resembled a shivering raisin. "Let's get outta this soup kid." And the two of them ran after the others.

* * *

"Come in, come in," said The Man. "Please dry yourselves off by the fireplace."

Ezra handed The Man his business card.

"I can't believe you're here. Part of me didn't think you even existed," said The Man, half to himself, as he read the card. And who could blame him. All the world had heard about the exploits of The 7 Policemen. Few had ever met these famous adventurers. But here they were now, standing in The Man's living room. Agathon, who had the strength of five men. Fauntleroy, the polyglot who could speak a hundred languages. Bjarne, the scientist who specialized in botany and chemistry. Teodor, who could solve any puzzle. Yoder, who knew things of magic and other dimensions that few could comprehend. And Ezra, their leader and chief strategist. The one who had saved their lives more times than anyone could count.

People never noticed that the famous 7 Policemen everyone talked about only totalled six. That was because no one ever remembered Frumbles. He had no special expertise. He had no amazing skills. He was the youngest of the group. And he was mostly afraid.

"Can we see the time machine Mister... uh, Mister Man?" asked Ezra.

"It's right this way," said The Man leading them to the small room. The time machine could barely hold The 7 Policemen. "I'm sorry about the tight squeeze officers," said The Man as he started pushing buttons and adjusting dials on the wall. "I never thought I'd have to transport so many."

"Do you remember the plan we discussed?" asked Ezra.

"Yes. I think so," replied The Man, still working quickly and still quite distraught over his missing son. "I'll send you back in time to about an hour BEFORE my son is to arrive in the past. You'll wait for him to appear and then bring him back to me."

"Morceau de gâteau." The Man turned to Fauntleroy. "That's French for 'piece of cake.'"

"I pray that you're right Officer Fauntleroy. Oh, I almost forgot!" The Man ran to a small table, opened a drawer, and brought out an odd-looking rectangular device: red with rough grooves, a toggle switch, and two lights. He handed it to Ezra. "This is a Time Phone. Hit the switch and you'll be able to speak to me wherever and *whenever* you are. As soon

as you find Grapecall, call me and I'll bring you back to the present time."

Ezra thanked him and put the phone in his pocket. "No pun intended, but it's time Mr. Man. Send us back so we can go get your son."

"Hold on one moment." It was Yoder. "Do you have a plastic bag?"

"Yes, I think so," said the man running to his kitchen and bringing back a small grocery bag from the supermarket. "Why do you need this?" he asked handing it to Yoder.

"You don't want to know Mr. Man. You just don't want to know."

3

Grapecall

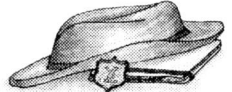

Grapecall was one of those few, rare individuals who was completely immune to the effects of time travel. No upset tummy, no dizziness, not even a wee bit of sleepiness. So after he found his ball and picked it up he ran out of the small bedroom completely unaware that he had traveled 80 million years back in time. Unaware that is until he looked around. His house was gone. He and the small bedroom stood atop a rocky cliff surrounded by shrubs. And when he looked over the cliff, all he could see for miles and miles were forests reaching out to the horizon in every direction.

The Sun shone down harshly reflecting off the metal of the time machine, blinding

Grapecall when he turned to look at it. He rubbed his eyes trying to adjust to the bright daylight, but when he opened them again the small bedroom was gone. Had he just seen the last bits of it fade away? He wasn't sure. He wasn't sure of anything.

Grapecall shouted into the hot sticky air. "Hello? Can anyone hear me? Is anyone there?" Only the sound of his own voice echoed back. So, with no one to ask for help, and no idea of where to go, Grapecall found a patch of moss and sat down. *I'll wait here for my Dad*, he thought. *He's probably looking for me right now.*

Grapecall thought about all the crazy inventions his dad had built over the years. The robot dog that cleans up after real dogs. Mixer boots that let bakers make batter with their feet. Camera gloves that take pictures of anything they touch. But none of those could have caused Grapecall to be in the predicament he was now.

Three hours passed. Grapecall was hot and thirsty. He knew he'd have to start looking for food and water soon. Where could his dad be? What was going on? And then, as if in answer to a prayer, a light rain started to fall. Grapecall opened his mouth, tilted his head back, and let the cool water fall into his mouth. But instead of seeing rain clouds, Grapecall saw a humongous dinosaur with a neck at least 40 feet long dripping saliva from its maw into Grapecall's mouth.

"Ewwww," he said spitting out the dino-slop. "What's a *Brachiosaurus* doing here unless...." And Grapecall knew. The small bedroom was the time machine his dad had mentioned. So Grapecall got up and started off to find food and shelter. The creature still slobbering spit onto his head wouldn't bother him as it was an herbivore and only interested in eating plants.

Grapecall was just about to start climbing down the cliff when he remembered the ball in his hands. He looked at this last remnant of the life he used to know and then, after wedging it under a nearby shrub, began his descent.

4
Rex

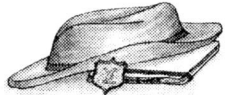

Ezra had a bad feeling. He felt as if he had thousands of teeny tiny dust mites dancing all over his skin, each little mite foot leaving just the tiniest scratch. He'd had this feeling many times before. And whenever he felt it, it usually meant something had gone terribly wrong.

"How long?" he asked Bjarne. "Uh, sixty-eight minutes," came the distracted reply. Bjarne was intensely studying the nearby shrubs, marveling at their amazing similarities to the plants from his own time. "These conifers could have been planted yesterday! I mean back in our own time. Just imagine, this same plant kept reproducing for tens of millions of years!"

Ezra chuckled. *Bjarne probably likes plants better than people*, he thought as he blew on his hands to keep them warm. He looked at the mist disappearing above his fingers and then for the twentieth time surveyed the desolate cliff upon which the time machine had deposited them. Trees stretching as far as the eye could see, and on the nearest foliage a thin frost. "Why is it that when you travel in time, the weather is never the same as when you left," he asked himself, partially for his own amusement, but mostly to give himself a break from the one nagging question that kept intruding on his thoughts. *Where was Grapecall?* If the policemen really did arrive in the past an hour before him, he should have arrived by now.

"How long?" Ezra asked again. "Sixty-nine minutes," answered the six slightly annoyed policemen.

The trip back in time had been unusual. Through the time machine's windows they had seen things they never thought they would see. An Elephant Bird. A Wooly Mammoth. Yoder swore that he had seen a bearded man in long robes shouting at them.

But Yoder had been busy evacuating the contents of his stomach most of the trip. Poor guy probably thought he saw lots of crazy things.

"Ezra! You've got to see this," shouted Bjarne excitedly.

"I really don't have time for a lecture on skunk cabbages Bjarne."

"No Ezra. You really DO need to see this." That was Teodor. And he was worried.

As Ezra ran over to where Bjarne and Teodor were kneeling, he saw what looked

like a ripped piece of blue cloth hanging from the underside of the shrub. Teodor lifted the corner and it crumbled to dust in his hand. He then rubbed the dust between his fingers and sniffed it. "If I didn't know better, I'd say this was some sort of rubber that decomposed. But that would be…." Teodor's face tightened. "Ezra, this is Grapecall's ball."

By this time the other policemen had joined them and the entire group was now covered in imaginary dancing dust mites. "Or to be more precise, this is what's left of Grapecall's ball after being left outside for many many years," continued Teodor. "We didn't travel far enough back in time. Grapecall is still further back in the past."

This was supposed to be a simple case. Go back in time. Get the boy. Bring him back to his father and have a nice dinner at home. Now dinner was going to have to wait. Ezra reached into his pocket, pulled out the Time Phone, hit the toggle switch, and put the phone to his mouth. "Mr. Man? Mr. Man, can you hear me?" For a very long ten seconds static came out of the phone's speakers. Then very faintly they heard, "This is The Man.

Your signal is very...." followed by a loud buzzing as if The Man had somehow turned into a giant bumblebee.

This was not good. "Mr. Man, if you can hear me, we need to go further back in time. Your son's not here. We're in the wrong time!" More crackles and hisses. And then a final reply. "...recalculate...send you... compartment..." The phone was dead.

Teodor took the phone from Ezra. "I'll try to fix it."

"Did you feel that?" asked Frumbles. "I think the ground shook."

They all felt it. Little tremors in the ground. Shake. Stop. Shake. Stop. Like a very large baby was quickly lifting the Earth above his head, pausing to smile, and then violently bringing it back down again. But this wasn't the work of a giant infant. Looking out over the forest Ezra could see trees falling in the distance. Was something knocking them aside? An animal perhaps? He could just catch glimpses of it. Faded green with gray markings. Running on two legs, but with really small arms. And are those teeth? Yes, definitely teeth. Lots and lots of teeth.

"Everyone back to the time machine. Now!" shouted Ezra as he and the other policemen started running as fast as they could.

"That was.... That was...." but Frumbles' lungs, bursting from the exertion, couldn't get the words out.

"A *Tyrannosaurus rex*," said Ezra completing Frumbles' sentence. "And he's in the mood for a seven course meal."

Indeed, things had gone terribly wrong.

5
Agathon

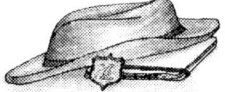

Teodor felt the air rush in through his nose. The little valve in his throat closing. The pressure building in his lungs. Had he held his breath 10 seconds? Thirty? Sixty? He slowly exhaled through his mouth and repeated the ritual again. And again. He knew when things were at their worst, when hope seemed like a bird that had flown away, when all you wanted to do was scream and cry, he knew these were the times that it was most important to keep calm. Focus on the task at hand. And find a way out of whatever terrible situation you were in. Trapped in a time machine he didn't know how to operate, 80 million years from the civilization he once knew, with a

Tyrannosaurus rex two minutes from eating him, Teodor slowed down his breathing in an attempt to calm himself down.

The time machine's control panel had at least 50 different buttons and knobs on a desk-like surface beneath three screens displaying mathematical equations. Symbols Teodor had never seen before were printed on each control and he feared he'd be leaving the *T. rex*'s digestive tract before he even learned how to turn the lights on in the time machine's cabin. If only Mr. Man were here to help. "Of course, that's it," he said to himself and then in a very calm clear voice Teodor looked right at the computer screen and said "Help."

"Please specify," replied a voice not unlike The Man's.

"Instructions on how to operate this time machine." Teodor's heart raced.

"Instructions displayed. Two thousand and thirty-seven pages."

The ground under the time machine started to shake harder. The roars of the *T. rex* grew louder. Teodor swiped his finger across the screen again and again trying to find the information that would save them. It all seemed like gobbledygook.

"Computer, engage autopilot. Send us back in time..." *How long? No time to figure this out. Just take a guess.* "100 years."

"Time travel must be performed manually."

"I need more time!" Teodor shouted.

Ezra, looking through one of the Time Machine's windows, could now see the *T. rex* clearly. They had maybe a minute at most. A meaty hand, the size of a small boy's head, rested on his shoulder. "I think maybe I go outside and play with lizard. Keep him occupied while Teodor get ship ready."

Ezra looked up into the smiling face of the largest man he'd ever known. Agathon was seven foot, eight inches tall and 360 pounds. Some said he had the strength of ten men, although in truth it was closer to five. As Ezra peered into Agathon's face, he realized he had never seen him frown. "No, definitely not. That *T. rex* has to weigh seven tons or more," said Ezra. "He'll crush you."

"If I not go, he eat ship." And with that Agathon bounded outside.

When Agathon was a boy—maybe seven or eight years old—he started climbing the mountains in his native Switzerland. On these expeditions he would take along a giant metal grappling hook that was attached to a rope the thickness of a man's wrist. Agathon would swing the grappling hook and throw it up the mountain where its pointy talons would sink into the rock face. He would then hoist his body up the rope, hand over hand, until he reached the grappling hook, pulled it out of the mountain's side and started the process again. Agathon loved climbing so much that no matter where he went, he always had his trusty grappling hook and a small pouch of chalk hanging from his belt.

As Agathon raced to meet the *Tyrannosaurus rex* he grabbed the small pouch and poured chalk onto his hands. *I will need to hold rope tight*, he thought as he looked over the cliff just in time to come face to face with a pair of four-foot jaws reaching out to cut him in half. Agathon dived as the jaws, swallowing only air, snapped shut with a terrifying clap.

The *T. rex* reached the top of the cliff and now bellowed above the policeman. Swinging his grappling hook in a circle above his head, Agathon replied, "You need to brush your teeth. Your breath smell like rotten egg."

The giant policeman let the grappling hook fly. It soared through the air straight at the dinosaur's leg. Straight at its leg until a tail the length of a small building intercepted it and the hook's sharp daggers sunk into dinosaur flesh. The *T. rex* screamed in pain, thrashing its tail up and down and pulling Agathon, who still held tightly onto the hook's rope, into the air.

Landing roughly on the *T. rex*'s tail, Agathon wrapped his massive arms and legs around the dinosaur's extremity. The *T. rex* twisted its tail back and forth trying to shake loose the grappling hook and its owner, but both held tight. Agathon wrapped the rope tightly around his arm. *I not lose best hook to*

this beastie.

Spying what looked like a large square rock out of the corner of its lizard-like eye, the *T. rex* smashed its tail into the side of the time machine. Agathon went flying, the force of his body pulling the grappling hook out of the dinosaur's tail. The time machine, six startled policemen inside of it, skittered down the side of the cliff, stopping on a small rock shelf a few feet below.

"Here beastie, beastie, beastie," called Agathon, the grappling hook once again swinging above him. The *Tyrannosaurus rex* turned and charged. But this time the hook, flying through the air once more, hit its target wrapping itself neatly around the dinosaur's legs. Rex fell to the ground, its weight creating a crater in the hard rock.

Ezra's voice cut through the air. "Agathon! We're leaving!"

"Not without my hook!"

Agathon jumped into the crater, grabbed his hook, and attaching it to a tree, threw the rope over the cliff wall and started climbing down. A little more than half way to the rock shelf he felt a tug on the rope and looked up to see the *T. rex* crushing the tree and grappling hook in its jaws. Jaws opened. Agathon fell.

A thunderous crash and all six policemen looked up to see a large bulge in the roof of the time machine.

"The *T. rex* is back!" yelled Frumbles.

"I don't think so," said Ezra as he opened the door and Agathon ran in.

"I dent roof."

Teodor started the time machine. Carousel lights. And The 7 Policemen disappeared just as Rex, fresh from sliding down the cliff face, stomped over to where the square rock was resting moments before.

6
Grapecalls

The sunlight felt good on Yoder's face. His mouth was dry, his joints ached, and if he moved as much as an inch, his stomach complained mightily. But at least he was out of that blasted time machine. Had he really seen what he thought he had? This particular trip through time had been especially rough on him and he wasn't sure he could trust his burning itchy eyes. But he knew, whether or not he had seen it, he needed to discuss it with Ezra.

"I'm telling you it is possible. I know what I heard." Fauntleroy was talking to Ezra as Yoder approached.

"What's going on?" Yoder asked.

"The *T. rex* spoke to Fauntleroy," Ezra said, his brow furrowing as if he were trying to decipher an impenetrable code.

"He spoke to all of us," insisted Fauntleroy. "The *T. rex* was shouting in some sort of dinosaur language. To your ears it probably sounded like the grunts and roars of an animal. But it had cadence, syntax, and structure. The *T. rex* was yelling. He was screaming as loud as he could, 'If I still had my powers, I'd turn you all into bugs.'"

No one knew more about languages than Fauntleroy. By the time he was 10 years old he could already speak twenty of them. By the time he was fifteen, he was inventing new ones. And because Fauntleroy had such vast linguistic knowledge, he could often start speaking a language he had never heard before just by listening to a few sentences of it. But talking dinosaurs? That sounded too fantastical.

Yoder, Ezra, and Fauntleroy stood silently for a few moments. No one knew what to say. Finally Yoder spoke. "I don't think that dinosaur was really a dinosaur."

Ezra and Fauntleroy both stared at Yoder.

"When I was watching Agathon fighting the *T. rex* I think I saw something. A faint aura—sort of a bluish-pinkish light—was surrounding the dinosaur. A magical aura. It was really weak—like the last light before day turns into night—but it was there. As if this was a magical creature who was losing its magic."

"A magical creature in the form of a *T. rex*?" asked Ezra.

But before the three policemen could discuss the matter further, Frumbles came running from the other side of the rock shelf. "Ezra, Yoder, Fauntleroy! Cavemen, coming our way!"

Sure enough, a small party of cavemen was making its way through the forest towards the cliff. Dressed in animal skins and holding spears the cavemen gestured excitedly towards the policemen and the time machine.

"Hello," Ezra called out to them. They grunted and shouted gibberish in reply.

Fauntleroy immediately let loose a low howl that seemed to come from the bottom of his stomach. He changed his posture to that of the cavemen, walking in a stooped position with his head thrust forward, as he shouted guttural noises that sounded like what Ezra imagined would be the result if an ape tried to imitate a pig. Out of the corner of his mouth Fauntleroy whispered to Ezra, "I told them that we were a tribe from far away and asked them who they are."

All six cavemen raised their voices in unison and uttered a single word. "Grapecall!"

"Ask again," Ezra told Fauntleroy. "Ask them what each of their names is."

Fauntleroy, speaking in the language of the cavemen, asked Ezra's question. Each caveman in turn shouted "Grapecall!" Six cavemen. Six Grapecalls.

"Fauntleroy, ask them if any of them are the son of The Man."

Fauntleroy howled and grunted. The cavemen's leader did the same. For a moment there was silence. And then all the cavemen ran back into the forest, disappearing inside the lush greenery.

"We are all sons of men," Fauntleroy

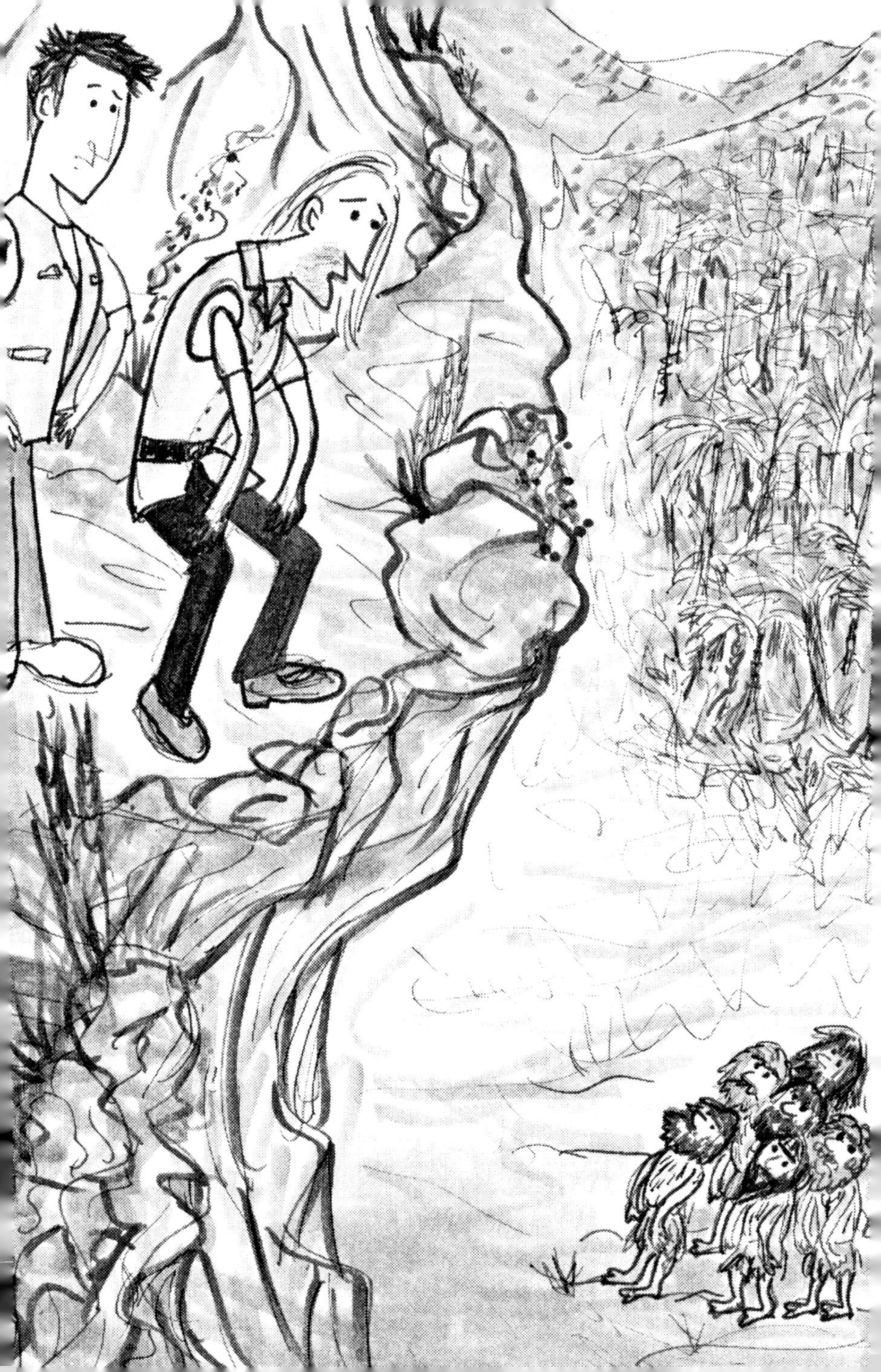

translated.

How could there be six Grapecalls? Why wasn't one of them a nine-year-old boy? And how were The 7 Policemen going to find the missing Grapecall and return him to his father? Ezra looked out over the forest wishing he could trade his time machine for a crystal ball.

7
Blue

They had started off easily enough. Built into the side of the cliff were steps that led down from the rock shelf to the clearing outside the forest. The forest itself, though thick with mammoth trunks, had plenty of room for the four policemen to maneuver through, with enough light coming through the spaces between the tree tops so they could make their way without mishap. But the forest soon turned into jungle. Agathon, leading the way, used his grappling hook to cut through dense vines and undergrowth as he slowly cleared a path for himself, Ezra, Yoder, and Fauntleroy. It wasn't quite pitch black, but the policemen could see no more than a couple of feet in any direction.

Ezra wondered if it had been a mistake to go after the Grapecalls. If they became lost in this harsh environment, they might never find their way back to the time machine. They'd be trapped in the past, just as The Man's son was.

But there was no other choice. The only way the policemen would be able to find The Man's Grapecall was through the other Grapecalls. They had to know more about The Man's son. After all, seven people with the same name couldn't be a coincidence. Could it?

Agathon stopped. The giant policeman, overheated and sweaty, took off his shirt and wiped some moss off the claws of his beloved grappling hook. "Which way we go now?"

Ezra looked around. Vines, trees, bugs, more trees, dirt, even more trees. And so little light, except for a bright shaft the width of a basketball that shot through an opening in the canopy of leaves above them. Ezra's eyes traveled up the beam of light until he saw a small patch of sky. Then he didn't. Then he did again.

"Follow those pterosaurs," he answered, pointing towards the last members of a flock passing by the opening in the jungle roof. "Hopefully they'll lead us to water. And where there's water, there may be a Grapecall."

As Agathon resumed hacking his way through the dense foliage, Ezra wondered how the other policemen back at the time machine were faring. Teodor, as brilliant as he was, had the unenviable task of trying to learn more about how the time machine operates. Sure, he had gotten them away from the *T. rex* by going further into the past, but he had no idea how many years back they had traveled, and even less of a clue about how he was going to return them to their own time. And, as if that wasn't enough, Teodor also had to figure out a way to fix the Time Phone.

Bjarne and Frumbles would try to take care of other matters while Teodor worked. Bjarne, with his knowledge of plants and chemistry, would look for food. If there was something safe to eat, Bjarne would find it. And Frumbles would assist Bjarne and Teodor any way he could. Frumbles may not have had any special skills. And he may have been forgotten by fans of The 7 Policemen. But he WAS one of The 7 Policemen, and he took that responsibility very seriously.

For a moment Ezra couldn't see. Blinding sunlight hit his eyes as he and his companions stumbled out of the forest into a grassy area surrounding a small lake. Odd birds swam across the placid water and dozens of snakes slithered nearby. As Ezra's eyes adjusted to the light he could see that across the lake was the entrance to a cave. The cave rested inside a hill that was solid rock and at least 50 feet tall. After their trek through the jungle, the four policemen could not imagine a more beautiful and peaceful sight. Then a scream pierced the silence.

They looked up to see a caveman on top of the hill flailing his arms wildly. He seemed terrified, his frantic grunts filling the air. Fauntleroy, who by now spoke fluent caveman, said, "He keeps shouting the word 'frog' over and over again."

A blue poison dart frog had jumped onto the caveman's arm. The caveman tried shaking it off, but as he did the frog jumped onto his face. He screamed yet again. He stumbled backward. And then he plunged over the side of the hill towards the ground 50 feet below.

8

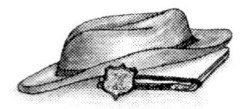

The Old Man

Agathon had many physical talents, but a fast runner he was not. So when he spotted the caveman atop the hill violently shaking his arm he did not hesitate. He ran, lumbering as fast as he could. Through the grassy field as Fauntleroy translated the caveman's grunts. Around the lake as the second scream cut through the air. Towards the rock wall as the caveman plunged downward.

Agathon lunged, twisting his body as he moved through the air. For just a moment he looked up at the sky, his back inches off the ground, his arms outstretched as if he were floating in a peaceful sea. It lasted for but a tenth of a second. And then the caveman landed on top of him.

"Oooof!"

Agathon's massive body had absorbed most of the impact, his powerful arms cradling the caveman's head, neck and torso and protecting them from the hard ground. But one of the caveman's legs was not so fortunate, hitting the earth with almost the full force of the fall. A loud snap rang out, as if a Cyclops had uprooted a tree and broken a thick branch in half to use as a toothpick. The caveman screamed his third and loudest scream. Looking down, Agathon could see a shard of bone protruding from the caveman's mangled leg.

"Don't move him," yelled Ezra as he and Fauntleroy ran over. The caveman started crying, trying to speak through deep sobs. Ezra examined the caveman's leg, hoping to locate the exact point where it broke. And Yoder appeared carrying vines and a splintered tree trunk. "I'm thinking if we can set the bone we can use these to make a splint."

All through this, Fauntleroy translated the caveman's words, although he had said one they all understood. "He says his name is Grapecall," Fauntleroy began. "But he also keeps saying we need to take him to Grapecall. The Grapecall inside the cave. I asked him why every caveman has the same name, but all he said was that every man is a Grapecall."

The caveman let out one final ear-shattering scream and then fainted as Ezra snapped his leg back into its proper position. He and Yoder used the vines to bind his leg to the tree trunk. Agathon lifted Grapecall off the ground and the four policemen headed into the cave.

The air inside the cave smelled sickly sweet from the dozens of half-eaten fruits that were strewn throughout the floor. Mosquitoes and flies buzzed everywhere. In the corner a creature resembling a cross between a hedgehog and a porcupine lay sleeping.

On the far side of the cavern was the opening to a passageway, a lit torch in a holder on the wall beside it. The width of the opening could barely fit a single man, so Ezra, grabbing the torch, led the policemen in single file.

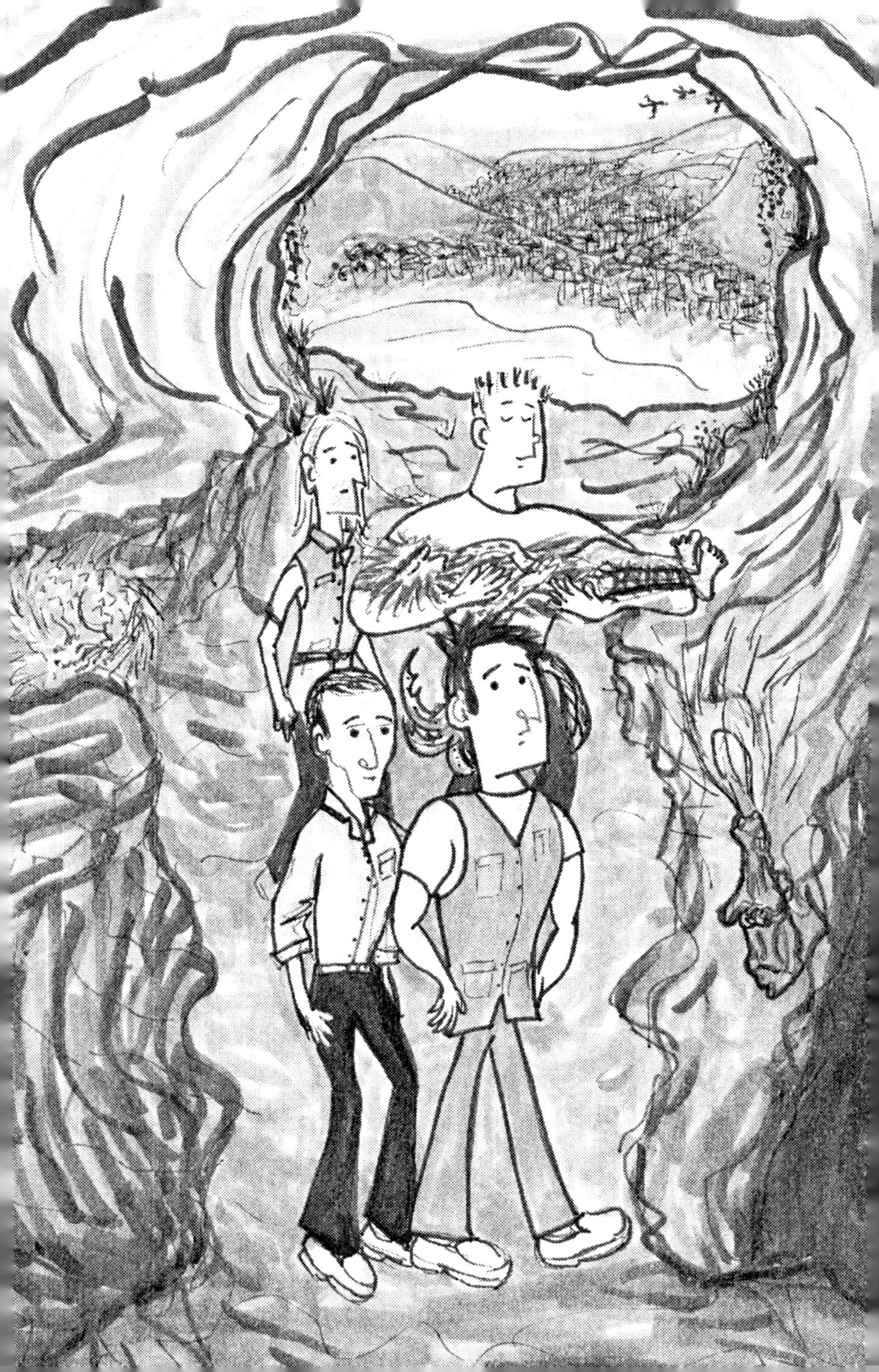

They walked through the gloom, only the crackling of the torch occasionally breaking the silence. Through the torch's dim light the policemen could see that the walls of the passageway were covered in tally marks. Thousands of hand-drawn five-line sets scratched into the rock walls. And as they walked further down the passageway, the tally marks grew fainter and fainter.

The passageway curved and the policemen

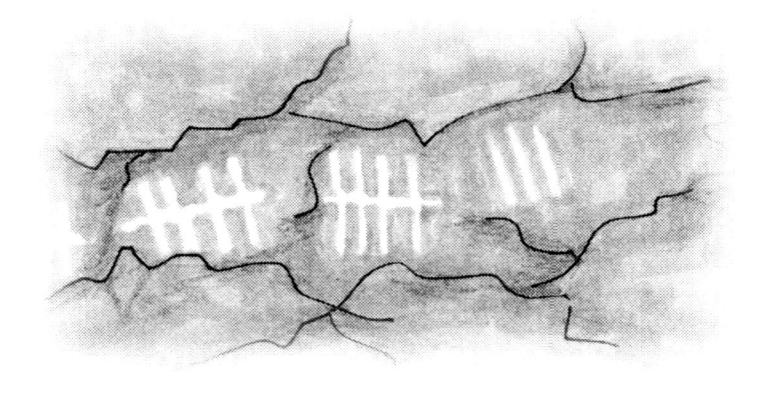

saw light coming through an opening up ahead. They entered a brightly lit chamber, its walls of metal ore reflecting light as if mirrors of every shape and size were built into the rock that surrounded them. A few feet away three cavemen were sitting in a semicircle. And within that semicircle, lying on the floor with his back propped against the wall, was a very very old man with a beard as long as a baseball bat. The old man raised his arm, and pointing a gnarled finger at the policemen, said in a very weak voice, "I know you."

"You're Grapecall, son of The Man?" asked Ezra, though he knew the answer before he even asked the question.

"Yes. I am," answered the old man. "I suppose the fact that I spoke English gave me away." He coughed weakly a few times. "And you're four of The 7 Policemen. I used to read about your adventures. But that was a lifetime ago."

Ezra and Fauntleroy started to walk toward the old man, but the three cavemen quickly leapt to their feet shouting angrily. The old man uttered a single word and the cavemen sat back down. "Friends," Fauntleroy translated. Then Agathon gently placed the Grapecall with the broken leg on the floor and all four policemen joined the semicircle around the old man.

The old man's beard was festooned with twigs, bits of fruit, dried honey, bark, dead bugs, pieces of meat, and blades of grass. The hides of animals, serving as blankets, were piled up on top of him. His skin looked paper thin.

"I am 96 years old today," the old man wheezed.

"The tally marks," said Ezra. "You've been keeping track of the days."

"Since the day I arrived."

"And the steps in the cliff. The torches on the wall. You made those," said Yoder.

The old man nodded.

"But why are all the other cavemen also called Grapecall?" asked Fauntleroy. "It's so confusing."

The old man laughed. "When I arrived here life was hard. I knew I wouldn't survive alone. So slowly, I organized the cavemen. Showed them how to make tools. Fire. Taught them whatever I could. I tried to teach them English, but they couldn't make the sounds. Except for one word: my name." The old man paused to cough again. He closed his eyes.

His voice became a whisper. "They thought since I was called Grapecall, they should all be called Grapecall. I never could explain to them why each of us would have a different name." His lips formed a slight smile.

"Tell me," the old man continued in a voice that could only be heard if your ear was to his lips. "How is my Dad?"

Ezra did not know what to say. The Man was terribly worried about his son. A son who was now older than his father was back in their own time. "He's well."

"Tell him," said the old man. "Tell him…."

For a moment all was silent. Then the three cavemen tilted their heads back and howled to the chamber's ceiling, their grief echoing off the walls as tears ran down their cheeks. Ezra bent over the old man's body, placing two fingers on the artery in his neck just under his jaw. There was no pulse.

Grapecall was dead.

9

Yoder

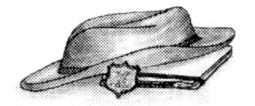

"So Grapecall is dead. But he's not dead." Frumbles was confused.

"He's dead in this time. *When* we are right now," said Ezra. "If we go back in time another 31,668 days, he'll be very much alive. And hopefully the exact same age as when he first entered the time machine."

"And how do you know that Grapecall arrived in the time machine 31,668 days ago?"

"He left us tally marks."

Indeed, Ezra, Yoder, Fauntleroy and Agathon had begun counting and recounting the tally marks as soon as they realized they had a way to figure out the exact day that

Grapecall had arrived in the past. And once they knew what that day was, the policemen could go back in time, retrieve the nine-year-old Grapecall, and return him to his father unharmed. At least that was the plan Ezra had just laid out for the other six policemen.

"Spaghetti," mumbled a very bleary-eyed Teodor. "Time is not like crossing from one side of a street to the other. It doesn't travel in a straight line. It's like spaghetti."

Teodor had spent the last 10 hours reading through the instructions on how to operate the time machine. He was irritable. He was tired. He was worried. His head was filled with strange equations. Impossible theories. Ideas that live in the gray area between magic and science. And Ezra just stood there looking at him. He cleared his throat and tried to speak a little clearer.

"Okay, let's back this up a bit. Imagine you have this really really long strand of spaghetti. You place it in a giant bowl all squiggly-like and you shake it up a bit. Then you climb a really tall ladder to look over the edge of the bowl. All you see are loops and loops of spaghetti. No beginning. No end.

That's time."

Frumbles was no longer the only one confused.

"Traveling through time is like following the path of that strand of spaghetti. You're zigging this way, zagging that way. You can't see what's up ahead and you can't tell where you are at any given moment." Teodor slouched into his chair in front of the time machine's control panel.

"So there's no button we can push that will send us 31,668 days further back into the past." Ezra gave his face a good hard rub. "And I imagine there's no button that will return us to our own time either."

"At best I can pick a direction—forward or backward in time—and estimate the point we should stop. Probably the only person who knows how to travel to an exact day in the past or future would be The Man. And he's millions of years in the future."

"Any luck with the Time Phone?"

"As far as I can tell, there's nothing wrong with it," Teodor sighed. "I tested it thoroughly. Every single circuit is processing correctly. It *should* work. It just doesn't."

Yoder turned to Teodor. "As if something was blocking the signal."

"Yes. How did you know?" But Yoder, now lost in thought, didn't answer. And for a long moment, all of The 7 Policemen remained still and quiet within the cramped confines of the time machine's cabin. Ezra, in a calm but determined voice, broke the silence.

"Teodor, get us as close to Grapecall's arrival date as you can." And then to the rest of the group he added, "Gather whatever food and supplies you can find. We'll leave as soon as Teodor's ready."

* * *

You'd think traveling through time would happen very quickly. Disappear in one time and reappear in another instantly. After all, wasn't that the point—to move through the centuries without having time actually pass? But one of the odd things about traveling through time is that *it takes time*. And never as much time as you'd think. One could travel a million years in a couple of minutes. Or ten days could take ten hours. There was no way to tell in advance.

This particular trip was taking *forever*. Yoder, sitting on the floor of the cabin, his faced pressed against a glass porthole, closed his eyes as his stomach churned. He remembered the first time he felt this way, as a small child in his father's car, going to see the Oracle. Up a hill. Down a hill. Round and round a mountain pass. Little Yoder threw up in his mother's handbag.

The Oracle wasn't at all what Yoder expected. Dressed in a denim shirt and pants, she wore her hair in pigtails that fell down to her knees. She greeted Yoder with a warm smile and together they drank tea as his mother and father answered questions about Yoder's birth and childhood. The tea settled his stomach and he felt a pleasant calm come over him.

But then the Oracle clasped her hands around his wrists and, turning his palms up, asked him to look into her eyes. When he did he cried out and turned his head. He tried to run away. The Oracle's grip was surprisingly strong, holding him in place with barely an effort.

"Have no fear. Look into my eyes. Look deeply."

Yoder looked again. The Oracle's eyes were missing. There were black holes where pupils and irises should be. But as he stared he could see within one of the holes a faint, flickering light. He leaned in. Closer. Closer. It was all there. The entire cosmos. The Solar System. The Milky Way. Galaxy upon galaxy contained inside the Oracle's head.

Yoder turned towards the other eye

socket. Within this one were walls of flame. And behind the fires, miles and miles of land populated by strange and powerful creatures. Yoder could feel the heat on his face as a creature, horse-like yet dripping with molten lava and with spikes shooting out from its hide, started galloping towards him. Faster and faster, barely noticing the tentacles of fire all around. The snout coming through the wall, smoke shooting out of its nostrils.

The Oracle released her grasp and young Yoder fell back into his chair. The creature was gone. And the Oracle now had eyes. Both of them brown.

"The child has the sight," she said. "He is in touch with the magical all around us. He can see it. It influences him. He can influence it."

Yoder returned from the land of his memories and opened his eyes. No longer reliving his childhood, he looked out the porthole at the colored lights that flew past like lightning bugs. So dark. So colorful. What was that? Darting between the lights. The bearded man in the long robes he'd seen before. And floating above him, way in the background. Is that the *T. rex*? The one Agathon had fought?

Blinding light forced Yoder to turn away. He felt dizzy and his stomach contracted. The time machine was slowing down. He turned back to the porthole and through it he could see below him, and in the distance, a very familiar forest.

The 7 Policemen stumbled out of the time machine into the fresh air. The trip had taken over five hours and they were stiff and tired. Teodor, hoping that the change in time would make a difference, tested the Time Phone, but it still wouldn't work. And Yoder, wondering if he had imagined seeing the robed man and the *T. rex*, sat down on the rock shelf to rest.

As Yoder looked at the time machine he was struck by how colorful it looked in the daylight. How all the lights swirled about it. *Lights? Swirling? Oh no. Please let this be my imagination*, thought Yoder. But the other policemen had seen it too. The time machine had vanished.

10

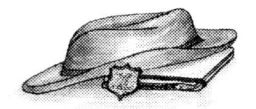

The Man

The Man sat in a dark corner of his living room, slumped in a chair, crying. For what he now saw before him was too much to bear.

In his mind he kept asking himself the same questions again and again. *How could I have been so stupid? Why did I do it? What did I think I would accomplish?* But the questions were there only to torture him. The Man had taken a tremendous risk and lost.

At first he had forced himself to be hopeful. *The 7 Policemen will be successful and return Grapecall to me in a little while*, The Man thought. *Everything will be fine.* But after hours of nervous waiting—when the Time

Phone finally did ring—there was no good news. Did the policemen say they were in the wrong time? When were they? All he heard was static. He tried to tell them what to do. How to recalculate the time stream. But he soon realized that his message never made it through. The Time Phone was dead.

The Man became frantic. He had to do something. But what? No one knew better than him how spaghetti-like time was. An hour of waiting for The Man could be three for Grapecall and The 7 Policemen. Or a minute. Or a year.

He needed information and there was only one way to get it. *There are 7 policemen*, he thought. *I have to assume that they are still alive. And if they're alive, they would always have at least one policeman inside the time machine trying to figure out a way home.* Before he could talk himself out of it, The Man pushed the big blue button.

This was all a few minutes ago, and now The Man sat crying as he looked at the empty time machine before him. Not one policeman had come back with it. And with no policeman to tell The Man what they had discovered, there was no way to figure out when Grapecall was.

Now eight people were stranded in the past. The Man, distraught, hung his head, letting the tears fall to the floor.

"I know you are heartbroken, but there is no time for that now."

The Man looked up. Someone stood in the other darkened corner of the room, a face concealed in shadow.

"Who's there?" he asked.

"A friend," said the stranger, walking into the light. Dressed in flowing robes, he was about the same height as The Man. And the smile behind the bushy beard and mustache was warm and genuine.

The Man peered deeply into the stranger's face. "You look so familiar. Do I know you?"

"We have met before, but that is not important now. Please take this." The stranger held out a scroll. "It contains the calculations for sending your time machine back to the exact date and time when the policemen will need it most."

"Why...." The man was having trouble

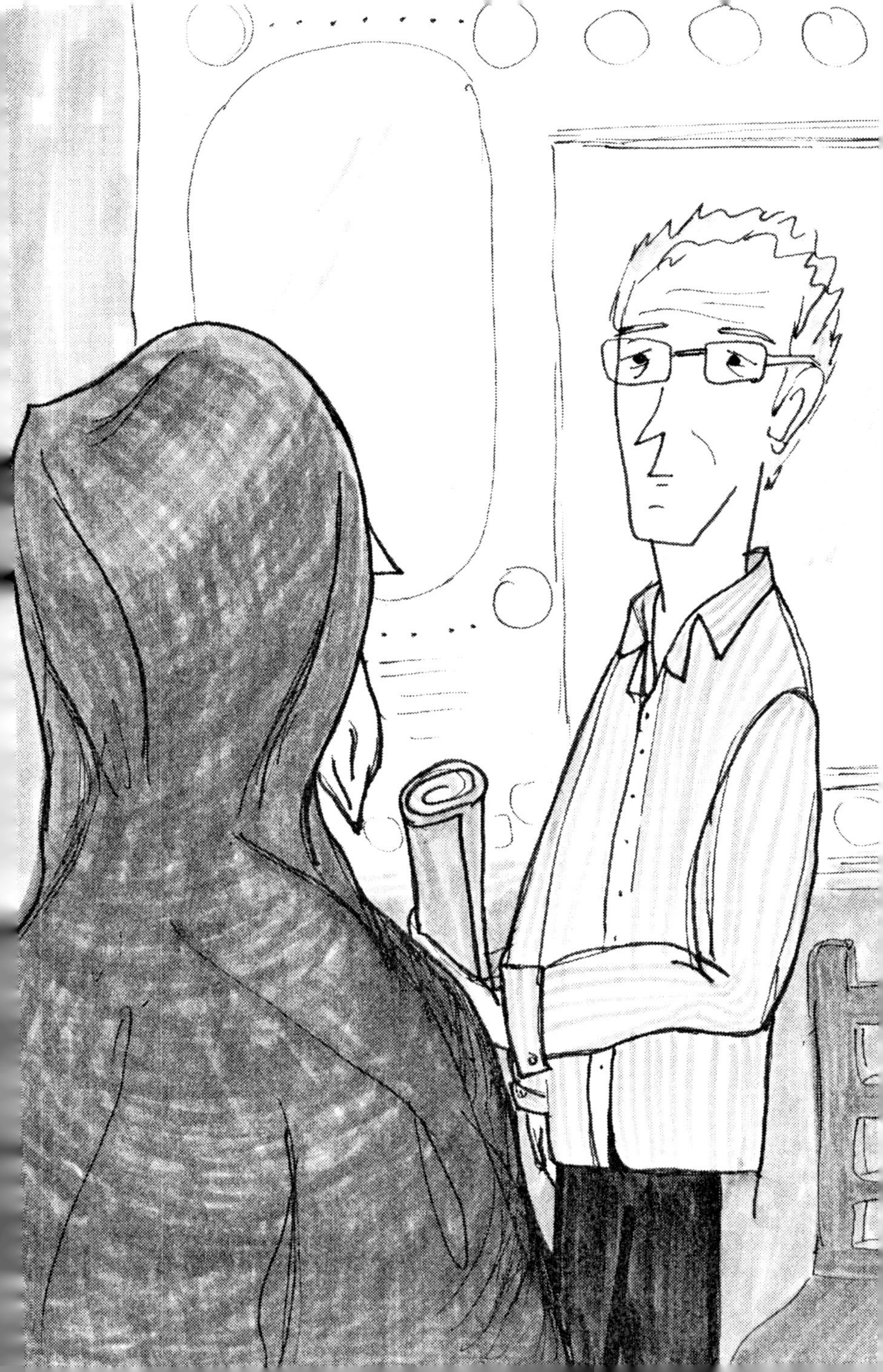

collecting his thoughts. "Why should I believe you?"

"If you don't, your son will be lost to you forever. And The 7 Policemen will be no more." The Man could see that the stranger was truly saddened by this thought. "Listen to your heart. It will tell you if I speak the truth."

"Grapecall deserved better than this," said The Man as he took the scroll from the stranger. "I should have been a better father to him."

"You are the best possible father he could hope for."

The Man just stared at the stranger as he stepped back into the shadow. "How do you know these things? Where do you come from?" he pleaded. "At least tell me who you are."

"To answer your questions would change your future." The stranger pushed a button on a small handheld device. "And you are the one person I would never lie to."

Swirling lights surrounded the stranger. Thirty seconds later he was gone.

11

Teodor

Teodor bounced the ball against the floor of the rock shelf and caught it. He bounced it again. And again.

"You had me climb mountain so you could play with children's toy?" Agathon asked as he finished descending from the top of the cliff where he had just retrieved Grapecall's cherished possession.

"It's more than a toy, Aggie. It's a marker in time. Grapecall didn't lose this ball. He left it for us to find. He knew it would tell us approximately how long ago he had arrived in the past." Teodor stared intently at the ball for what must have been the fiftieth time. "When we found it the first time it had turned to dust because it had been sitting outside for almost 200 years. But now...." Teodor's voice trailed off.

Agathon motioned for Teodor to throw him the ball. What seemed large in Teodor's hands now resembled an oversized marble in Agathon's. The giant policeman examined the ball and smiled. He understood. "It still inflated," he said.

"Yes, it hasn't lost much air. Its color hasn't faded from exposure to sunlight. And it hasn't been outside long enough for the surface to get hard and brittle. That ball—Grapecall's ball—is still fairly new." Teodor looked up into Agathon's hopeful expression. "I think our nine-year-old is still nine years old. And I think he hasn't been in the time of the dinosaurs long. If we're lucky Aggie, Grapecall's nearby and unharmed."

"You become optimist!" kidded Agathon, who loved joking about how much the two policemen were alike. But in truth, Teodor and Agathon were a study in opposites. Where Agathon would rush into danger without hesitation, Teodor would make a plan. Where Agathon trusted his instincts,

Teodor only trusted facts. Agathon was the tallest policeman. Teodor was the shortest at 5' 2". Agathon loved talking to strangers, going to parties, and telling stories. Teodor liked reading stories *about* strangers and parties. But despite these and hundreds of other differences great and small, Teodor and Agathon were the best of friends.

The two had met under terrible circumstances. The 7 Policemen were investigating a case concerning the disappearance of a brilliant mechanical engineer who had invented a device that could stop sound. Put the device in a room, flick the switch, and talking would not be heard. Feet stomping on the ground would be silent. Music playing from speakers would evaporate into nothingness.

Agathon had tracked the engineer to a secret laboratory inside a dormant volcano. But when he burst through the laboratory door, the engineer was seated, calmly eating a sandwich. No one had kidnapped him. No one had forced him to leave. The engineer simply wanted to get away from all the people demanding to use his sound stopping invention.

But before Agathon could learn more, an earthquake shook the laboratory's walls down upon them. He and the engineer were trapped in an air pocket surrounded by tons of volcanic rock. The oxygen wouldn't last long. And it would be days before a rescue team could dig them out.

Agathon and the engineer sat amid the wreckage of the laboratory for a few minutes, each deep in his own thoughts. Finally, the engineer broke the silence. "I suppose I should formally introduce myself," he said. "I'm Teodor. And I think I have a way for us to escape."

Teodor explained that the pieces of volcanic rock all around them started as lava that erupted out of the volcano in the middle of the last ice age. The extreme cold caused the molten lava to turn into rock very quickly, trapping small amounts of oxygen within each piece. If Agathon could break open the rocks, that might release enough oxygen to keep them alive while Teodor worked on the second half of his plan.

As Agathon started smashing rock

after rock with his grappling hook, Teodor proceeded to take apart the invention that started this awful adventure. His plan was to convert it from a device that stops sound to one that shoots sound. A lot of sound.

For hours Teodor worked. And for hours Agathon smashed rock after rock, releasing precious life-giving oxygen into the air. But Agathon tired. His muscles ached. And despite his efforts, there just wasn't enough air in the rocks to keep them alive much longer.

Barely able to breathe, Teodor ripped the sleeve off his shirt and, separating it into four pieces, the two men fashioned earplugs for themselves. Teodor turned on his reconfigured invention and the noise was deafening. But after adjusting its settings, a large powerful bubble formed around them. Inside the bubble Teodor and Agathon heard nothing. But outside it, waves of vibrations caused by the device's noise moved anything in its way. So slowly, encased in this sphere of noise that protected them from the rocks above, Teodor and Agathon used the new invention to clear a path before them as they walked through hundreds of feet of volcanic rock to the safety of a warm spring day.

Soon afterward, Teodor joined Agathon as one of The 7 Policemen. And through many adventures their friendship deepened. But now, Teodor wondered if this would be their last adventure together. Yes, they might finally find Grapecall. But in his heart he was terrified. He knew that they were trapped in the past with no way to get home.

* * *

Frumbles' brow was dripping with sweat. While the rest of the policemen were trying to stomach the roots and herbs Bjarne had gathered, he was furiously shaving the bark off a branch and carving the end to a sharp point.

"Nice," remarked Yoder, examining one of the many others Frumbles had already finished.

"I made a bow too Mr. Yoder." Frumbles motioned to a rock upon which laid another branch bent into the shape of the letter "c" with a thin vine tied between the two ends. Yoder picked up the crude bow and pulled back the vine. Upon release, it snapped back into place with surprising force. Yoder put the bow down next to Frumbles.

"I told you before kid. Don't call me Mr. Yoder," Yoder told Frumbles not unkindly. "I'm just Yoder." But before Frumbles could explain that he addressed everyone formally when he was nervous (which was most of the time), Ezra called the two policemen over to where the rest of the group had gathered.

"Gentlemen," Ezra told the assembled

policemen, "Teodor says that Grapecall may have come to this time only a few days or weeks ahead of us. Certainly no more than six months. We'll make one last attempt to call The Man on the Time Phone, and if it's still not working, we'll set off and search for Grapecall on our own."

Ezra nodded and Teodor reached into his pocket for the Time Phone. But when "the man who could solve any problem" looked at what he brought out, he was confronted by a problem he could not solve. The Time Phone had been replaced by a brick. A brick inscribed with a message:

> RETURN TO THE CAVE OF THE OLD MAN
> THERE YOU MAY FIND
> THE ANSWERS YOU SEEK

The last thing The 7 Policemen needed was another mystery, let alone one this strange. Looking down at the brick, Ezra could only say, "Let's go."

* * *

The descent down the side of the cliff had been extremely difficult. More than once Agathon found himself lunging for a policeman about to fall off the rock wall as he desperately hung onto his grappling hook with his other hand. Those steps carved into the cliff would have made their journey much easier. But they would not be built for several decades. And only if The 7 Policemen failed in their quest to rescue Grapecall.

The forest too was different. Creepy. As if they were walking through a picture of a forest that looked exactly like what you'd expect, except for some missing ingredient. Yoder motioned for the group to stop.

"It's the animals."

"What animals?" asked Ezra. "I don't hear any animals."

"Exactly."

The last time Ezra and Yoder had been in this forest if was full of life. But now all was silent. No snakes slithered. No wings fluttered. Nothing jumped from branch to branch. The only sound was the soft breathing of The 7 Policemen.

"Did you see that?" Bjarne was pointing to the ground. "I swear the dirt right there moved. Just a tiny bit."

"Could be worm, maybe?" offered Agathon.

Bjarne knew that what he saw could not have been caused by a worm. The topsoil, about a circle six inches across, seemed to jump up imperceptibly. As he stared at the spot where the earth had moved it happened again. But this time all the soil moved. And all the policemen felt the vibrations that accompanied it. Boom. Boom. Boom. Something big was coming. Getting closer. And fast.

"This way," whispered Ezra, and, as if they were of a single mind, the policemen started running in a single line, retracing their steps back the way they had come through the forest. Turning off the path the group came to a giant redwood, eight feet around, that had fallen and now provided a high enough wall to hide the policemen. They jumped over it and waited.

The ground shook violently accompanied by the sounds of falling trees. A caveman, weak and out of breath, stumbled feebly past them. And then the creature appeared. Teeth glistening. Roar deafening. It stopped twenty feet away, turning its head in the direction of the hidden policemen. Peeking over the edge of the fallen tree, they saw a terrifyingly familiar face.

"I will play with beastie again. You go to safe place."

"No," Yoder whispered. "His aura is powerful! His magic...." But Agathon had leaped over the tree and was already running towards his old friend.

"Here beastie, beastie, beastie," he shouted, swinging his grappling hook over his head. But when Agathon looked into the *T. rex*'s eyes he saw two red glowing embers alternating from soft to bright over and over again, as if a small child were playing with the dimmer on a lamp. Agathon gasped as bright red rays shot out from those embers engulfing his body in light.

From behind the fallen tree the other policemen watched as Agathon dropped his grappling hook and fell to the ground. The beams from the *T. rex*'s eyes intensified. Agathon's clothes dissolved. His skin turned white. Fur sprouted over his entire body. He became a polar bear. No, not a polar bear. He was shrinking. Smaller. Smaller. A rabbit? No, smaller still. A naked mole rat? No, even smaller. Something the policemen could barely make out. The ray beams stopped. The *T. rex* roared. Agathon had been turned into a glowworm.

For the first time in his life Teodor did not think. He did not plan. He jumped over the fallen tree and ran to his friend. He would not leave Agathon to be stomped into the ground by that prehistoric beast. But as the valiant policeman raced through the trees, he too fell victim to the *T. rex*'s eye beams. And the five remaining policemen, for the second time, watched in horror as one of their own changed before their eyes. Teodor had been transformed into a puny tortoise.

12

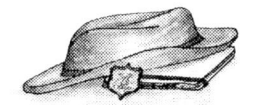

Frumbles

Frumbles shook uncontrollably. He pressed his back against the trunk of the felled tree, wrapped his arms around his knees, and buried his head in his chest. He was certain that he would be the next one caught in the *T. rex*'s eye beams. That he would be turned into something horrible. A woodchuck. Or a slug. Quite possibly a dung beetle.

The roars of the dinosaur hurt his ears and Frumbles wished he had never joined The 7 Policemen. Why *did* he join? When Mr. Yoder showed up at his front door with his offer to become a member of the most famous group of adventurers the world has ever known, it seemed so peculiar. He didn't have any special skills. He didn't like putting his life in danger. He was Frumbles the librarian. Nothing more. Everyone knew that.

But the way Mr. Yoder said "We need you kid" made him feel like this would be the most important thing he could do with his life. So for the last two years Frumbles followed the policemen from one adventure to the next. Always trying to be helpful. Never quite fitting in. And sometimes feeling very much in the way.

Now Frumbles only felt fear.

Suddenly, the sound of running. Heavy feet off to the side crunching leaves and snapping twigs. From the corner of his eye Frumbles could see Yoder making for a large sycamore far to the right of the *T. rex*, two columns of red light barely missing him as he dove behind the tree. And then Yoder's body swinging to the other side of the sycamore as the eye beams, having bounced off a puddle on the ground, missed him a second time.

Rex, head down, charged Yoder's tree, each step creating clouds of dust and shaking loose from the foliage above a steady rain of branches, leaves, bugs, nests, snakes,

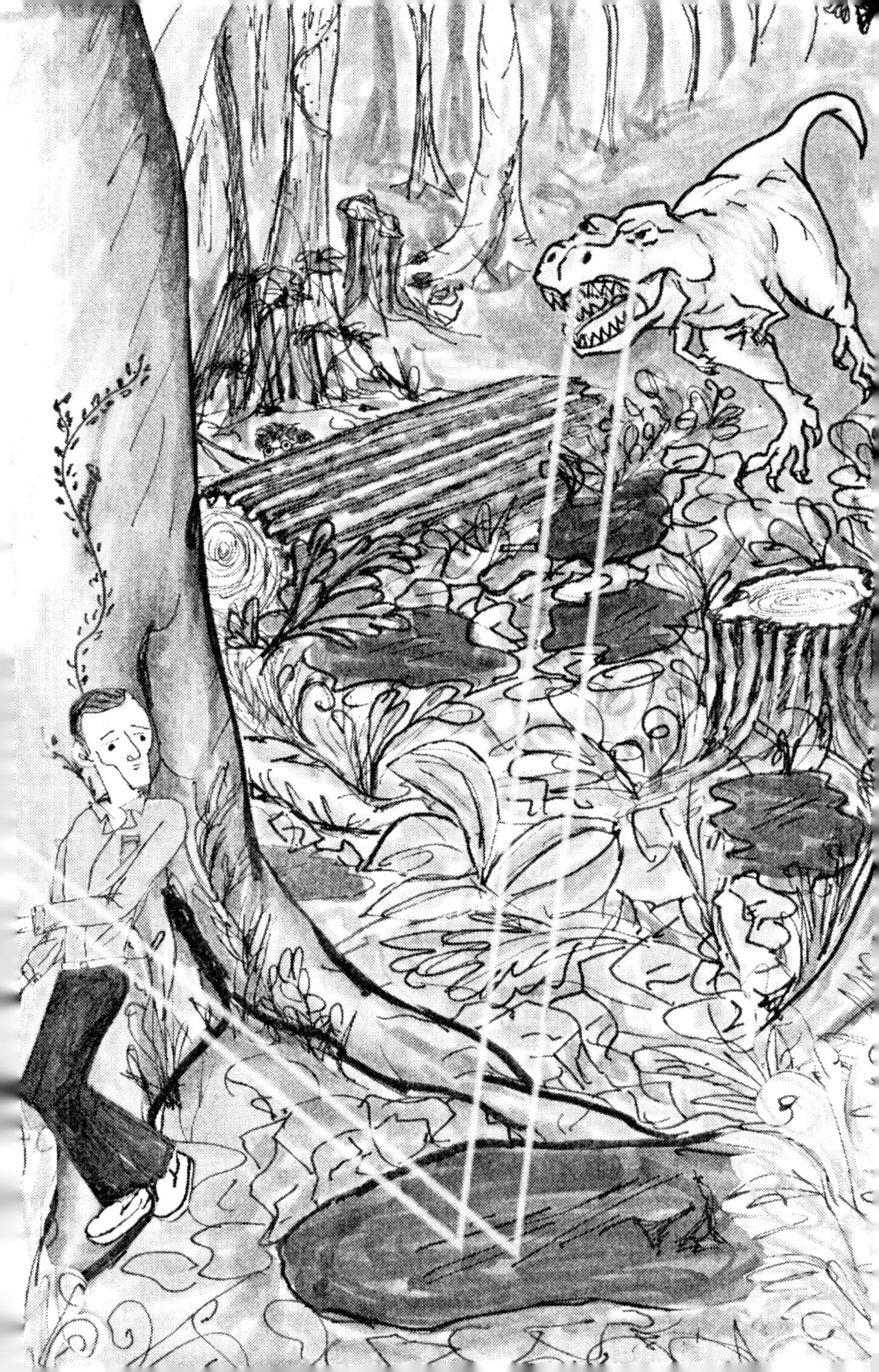

and frogs. Yoder, face to bark, watched the rampaging creature head his way. He stood motionless, the only exception his moving lips, talking to no one but himself.

"Yoder, Run!" shouted Frumbles, forgetting his fear. "Run!"

But Yoder held his ground. Soon the creature would smash into the tree, the trunk falling to the ground and crushing Yoder beneath it. Frumbles cringed, the inevitable death of his friend seconds away. Inevitable, were it not for the cantaloupe-size stone that flew through the air and collided with the dinosaur's skull seconds before it reached Yoder.

The *T. rex* reared back and whirled around just in time to see Ezra throw another stone that missed him by inches. Forgetting Yoder, Rex opened its jaws wide and let loose an ear-piercing yell as he barreled towards the lone policeman. Ezra turned and ran, but without any real shelter nearby, he knew that he barely had seconds before he became a crunchy treat for the angry creature pursuing him.

Frumbles, no longer afraid for himself,

frantically looked around for a stone, a stick, anything he could throw to distract the beast away from Ezra. Something snapped under his foot. An arrow, next to several others.

Frumbles had never shot an arrow before. He had never used a bow. In fact, he was surprised he was even able to make one, having done so only in the hope that one of the other policemen would be able to use it. But now, without thinking, with only the urgent hope to save Ezra's life, Frumbles grabbed the bow, notched an arrow, and let it fly towards the beast's tail. It sank deep into the dinosaur's flesh.

Then, as Frumbles would later describe it, something very strange happened to him. All sound, all movement, everything, it all slowed down. The roars of the beast became low and muffled. The beams shooting from its eyes hung in mid-air while Frumbles stepped aside to dodge them. And the bow, this formerly strange device, became amazingly comfortable within his grasp. As if he had been an expert archer his entire life. As if he was born to this.

So, undisturbed by his surroundings,

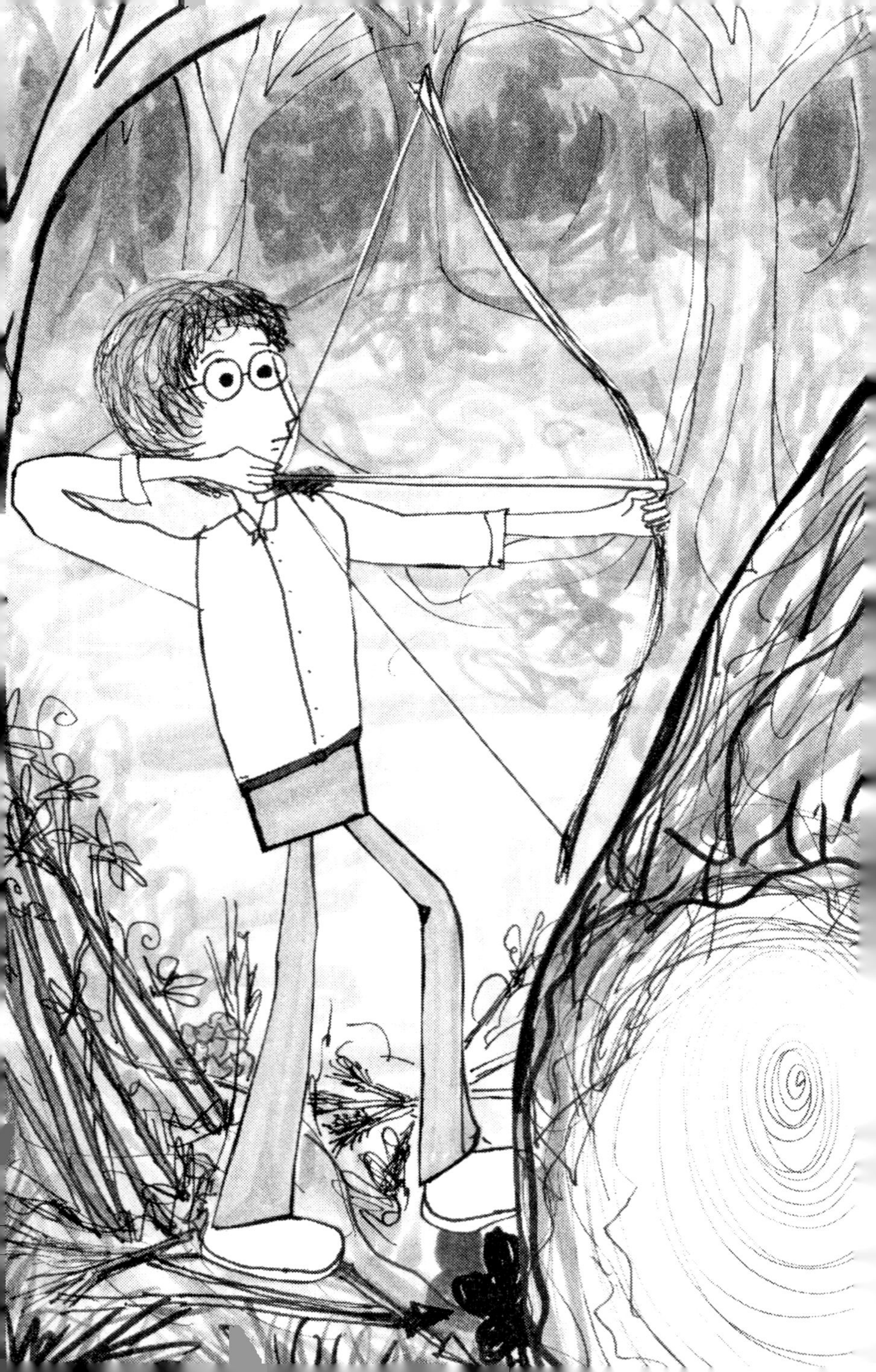

Frumbles picked up three arrows, held two in his teeth and fired the first. He slid the second out, sending it on its way. And released the third into his waiting hand to soon join its brothers in the air. All three arrows hit the dinosaur's arm, pinning him to a tree.

"Time to go kid." It was Yoder. The slow motion of sight and sound had stopped. The screams of the creature were back. Ray beams nearly hit them as Yoder pushed Frumbles down behind the tree.

"What about Agathon and Teodor? We can't just leave them." Frumbles looked like he was about to cry as Yoder pulled him farther away from the *T. rex*, who was struggling mightily to free himself.

"Wrong question kid." Yoder smiled. "You really should be wondering what Bjarne and Fauntleroy have been up to."

13

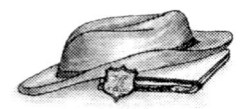

Bjarne

Ezra waited. He had waited while Bjarne stared at moss. At spiders. At bat droppings. At mushrooms. At so many other things. And now he waited while Bjarne stared at the roots of a tree. Judging by the position of the Sun, he had been waiting at least a couple of hours.

"Let me see how he's doing," Ezra whispered, hoping not to disturb the botanist too much.

Bjarne absentmindedly reached into his shirt pocket and handed Ezra what could have been mistaken for the world's smallest flashlight. Except this flashlight wiggled.

"Hang on Agathon. We're working on a

way to get you back to the way you were," Ezra told the much changed policeman.

So far the plan had worked. While Ezra and Yoder (with the unexpected and miraculous help of Frumbles) distracted the dinosaur, Fauntleroy scooped up tortoise Teodor and Bjarne grabbed glowworm Agathon, the grappling hook, and Agathon's chalk bag. With the policemen safely away from the *T. rex*, Fauntleroy, Yoder, and Frumbles headed off to the cave of the Old Man to wait for Ezra and Bjarne, who would join them as soon as part two of the plan was finished. Unfortunately, part two wasn't going so well.

"Maybe if you told me what one looked like I could help you find it," urged Ezra as he slipped his mountain climbing glowworm friend into his own pocket.

Bjarne could tell that the chief policeman's patience was coming to an end, but he didn't want to alarm Ezra. He didn't want to tell him that the mystical Plape Leaf, the one thing that Yoder said might restore Agathon and Teodor back to human form, and the one thing they had been looking for these last two hours, was something he could not describe. For Bjarne had never actually seen one.

"The Plape Leaf is kind of hard to pin down," Bjarne answered, still staring at the tree roots. He took a deep breath. "It's hard because it might not actually exist."

Ezra sat down on the ground crushing an anthill with his bottom. As hundreds of ants tried to escape the giant creature that just obliterated their home, he wiped his forehead with the sleeve of his shirt. It would be night soon and Ezra did not want to be in this forest after dark.

"Let me guess. There's an ancient scroll."

"An entire book actually!" Bjarne was never more excited than when he got an opportunity to talk about plants. "Written over twenty-five-hundred years before our time, it tells of a miraculous leaf with incredible medicinal powers. The Greeks described it as 'The hand of the healing spirit.' And Yoder said there was magic in the ground near here. So we thought...."

Ezra shook his head. Had they been wasting valuable hours that should have been spent trying to get back to their own time? Maybe, but he understood Bjarne and Yoder. He did not want to give up on trying to help Teodor and Agathon either. Making matters worse, Ezra and Bjarne were now drowning in a sea of ants as thousands of the six-legged creatures continued to pour forth from the crushed anthill.

"You must have *some* idea what to look for?"

"The ancient text says 'where nature is disturbed and patterns arise you will find the Plape Leaf, for its magic is the cause,' " Bjarne explained.

"You have no idea what that means, do you?"

"None whatsoever." And with that Bjarne brushed a few hundred ants off a rock and sat down as well.

Bjarne, Ezra, and at least ten thousand ants watched the fading light of the day come through the canopy of leaves above them. *If it wasn't for the terrible predicament we're in, this would be quite lovely*, Bjarne thought. And then a moment later, another thought.

"I have not gotten one ant bite. Have any bitten you?" Bjarne asked. "You crushed their home. Normally they would be quite annoyed. And how come none of them are crawling on us?"

As Bjarne had suspected, Ezra had not received a single bite. And as they could both plainly see, every one of the insects was being careful to avoid them. But when Bjarne took a closer look at the ants he gasped. The tiny creatures had formed circles. Hundreds of them. Each with twelve ants marching around and around. The floor of the forest looked like it was covered with miniature bicycle wheels, each perfectly the same size, turning and turning endlessly.

"Nature disturbed. Patterns arise," Bjarne, whispered to himself in astonishment. Then almost shouting, "Ezra!

The ants! We need to dig. Right here!"

The two policemen dived into the middle of the ant sea and using their hands frantically began clearing away the dirt on the forest floor. Digging and digging, throwing handful after handful of soil to the side, the hole became big enough so that only their heads could be seen as they worked. And then, just like in a puppet show, their heads went straight down and disappeared.

Bjarne and Ezra were falling through the air in an underground chamber, the floor of the hole having crumbled under their weight. Water hit Ezra hard and seaweed wrapped around him as he plunged deep into some sort of marsh. Struggling through the underwater plant life he pushed to the surface and, gasping for breath, called for Bjarne. There was no reply.

The chamber was dark and Ezra could barely see two inches in front of himself. Remembering Agathon, he quickly floated on his back, reached into his shirt pocket, and desperately felt for the policeman. He brought out the small creature. It no longer glowed, but it moved ever so slightly. Ezra hoped Agathon was alright, placed him on top of his head, and resumed dog paddling.

"Bjarne! Bjarne!"

Only echoes came back to Ezra's ears. *Did Bjarne hit a rock when we fell? He could be injured. Or worse. If only there was some light. What's that coming up from the water? Purple and green and orange.*

Bjarne burst from the water, each hand glowing with bright multicolored lights. Ezra grabbed Bjarne and little sparks from Bjarne's hands stung Ezra in the face. No, not his hands. Each of Bjarne's fists held five or six large leafy glowing plants that shot little electric jolts into the air.

"Plape Leaves!" shouted Bjarne triumphantly.

* * *

Thanks to Agathon's grappling hook Bjarne and Ezra had been able to climb out of the boggy marsh and up the wall of the underground chamber to the forest above. But now night had fallen and the two policemen felt relief as they pushed through the edge of the forest and saw the Old Man's cave on

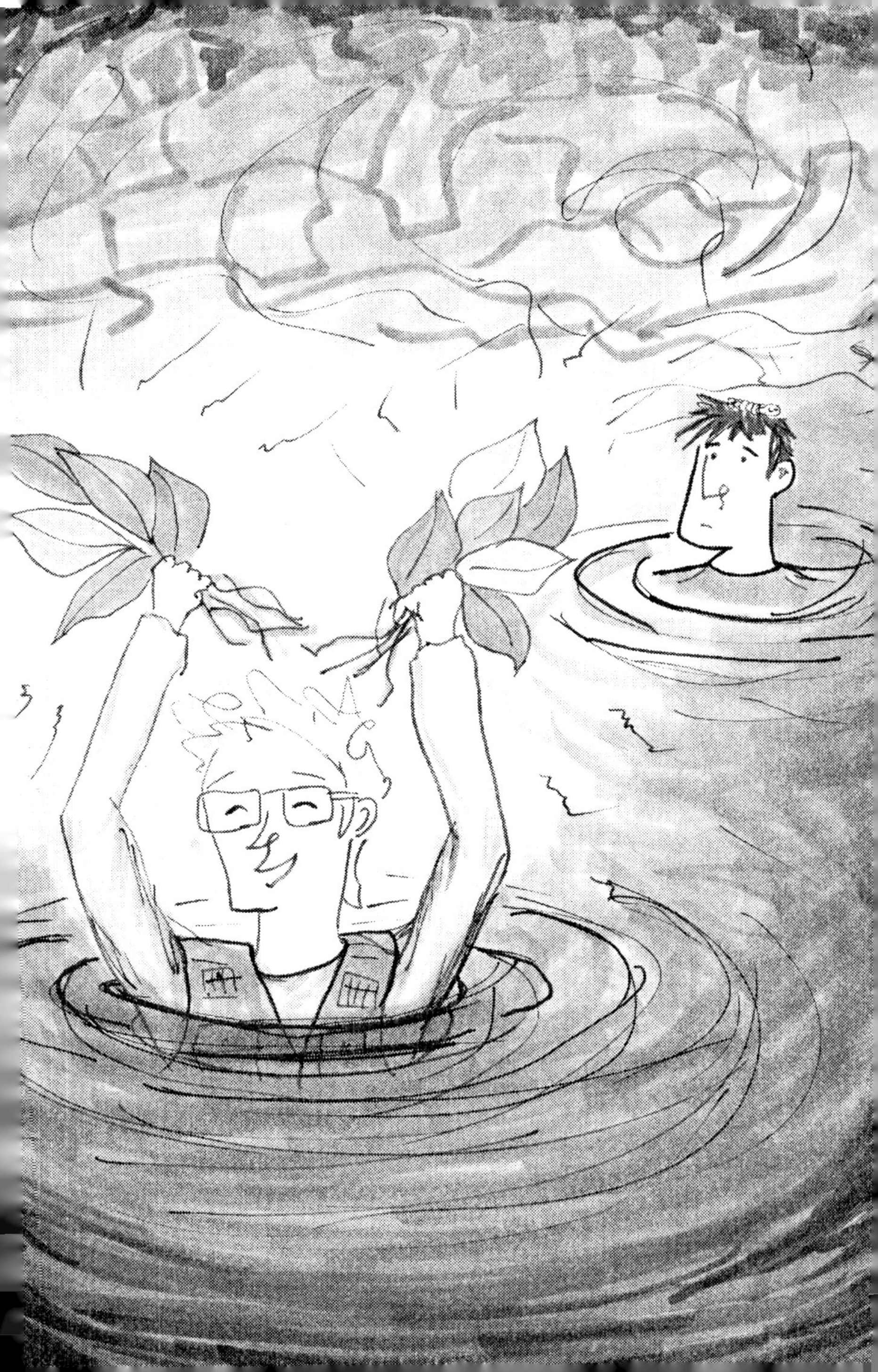

the other side of the lake. Upon entering the cavern, Bjarne and Ezra were startled to see a creature that looked like a cross between a hedgehog and a porcupine sleeping soundly in the corner.

Quickly crossing to the far side of the cave, Bjarne entered the passageway followed by Ezra. Using the Plape Leaves to light the way, the two policemen made their way through the dank darkness.

"Stop," Ezra called out. Something was on the wall, but they couldn't quite make it out. Taking Agathon from the top of his head, he held the glowworm up to the stone. At first, Agathon did not glow. But as Bjarne brought the Plape Leaves closer to the transformed policeman, Agathon started to wiggle. Just a little. Then a little more. And then the little glowworm erupted, shining a strong beam that revealed twenty-two tally marks.

The passageway curved and Bjarne and Ezra saw light up ahead. A small fire was burning in the chamber as they entered and there stood Yoder, Frumbles, and Fauntleroy. The three policemen parted and behind them Ezra and Bjarne could see a small nine-year-old boy wearing a bark and wood hat and playing with a blue ball.

14
Fauntleroy

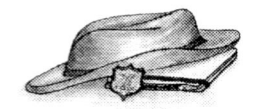

It should have taken a minute. No more than two. But glowworm Agathon and tortoise Teodor had been eating the Plape Leaves for an hour and they were still glowworm Agathon and tortoise Teodor.

After the first five minutes Yoder knew something was wrong. But even with his magical sight, he could not detect why the Plape Leaves did not work. So he sat down on the cave floor, closed his eyes, and to Grapecall's surprise, went to sleep. But the policemen knew this wasn't quite what it appeared to be. Yoder was actually entering a state of "ethereal gathering." Although his body was inactive, his thoughts flew across the earth searching for and collecting magical energy. Energy he hoped would help Agathon and Teodor. Unfortunately, no one ever knew when Yoder would wake up. It had been an hour. He might stay "asleep" for days.

Ezra was growing impatient. "Maybe they're not Plape Leaves," he suggested. He examined one in his hand as it gave off a little spark. "Plenty of creatures in nature manufacture light. This could be some prehistoric plant we've never seen before."

"Oh, those are most definitely Plape Leaves," Bjarne replied. "When I fell into the marsh I was drowning. Swallowing water and sinking to the bottom fast. My body went cold and I closed my eyes. I thought 'This is the end of me.' Then I had no more thoughts. But when I opened my eyes my lungs were clear. I was warm and comfortable. And I was *breathing underwater*. I didn't know how that was possible until I looked down and saw I had landed on those glowing plants."

Putting the leaf down, Ezra looked as his reflection in the cave wall. He was exhausted. Hungry. His head ached with questions. Would Agathon and Teodor ever be human again? What did the future hold for us? Would we all live out our lives in the cave as the old man did? Five policemen raising a nine-year-old boy in prehistoric times? If things weren't so grim, Ezra would have chuckled at the absurdity of it.

The sound of coughing jolted Ezra out of his reverie. It was Yoder coming out of his trance. Weak and not yet able to speak he motioned towards Agathon and Teodor. Frumbles and Fauntleroy each grabbed one of his arms, and supporting Yoder's weight, helped him walk to the glowworm and tortoise.

In a crackly voice Yoder whispered, "Hold them up to the light."

Ezra picked up the two transformed policemen and raised them up to a torch.

Yoder smiled as if he was in the presence of unbelievable beauty. "Son of a magi."

"Son of a magi" was an expression Yoder reserved for moments of great emotion. Sometimes he used it to vent anger. Or frustration. But this time he said it as if he had been blind for a hundred years and then suddenly regained his sight. Which was kind of what happened, for upon awakening from his ethereal gathering, Yoder's magical sight was increased a hundred fold. He could now see thousands of intricately spun threads of magic surrounding and wrapping around Agathon and Teodor.

"It's a magical prison," Yoder told the rest of the policemen and Grapecall as he drank some water peppered with leaves and nasty looking roots. It tasted like sweaty socks that had been buried by a dog, but Bjarne said it would give him strength. "A prison constructed by our friend to block any magic that would restore Agathon and Teodor back to their human forms."

"Our friend?" Frumbles asked.

"I'll give you one hint," Yoder replied. "His name starts with a 'T' and ends with a 'Rex.'"

No one said a word. None of the policemen liked the idea of going up against the prehistoric monster again. They had barely escaped with their lives twice. After a while, a small voice spoke.

"I will fight the *T. rex*. I'm not exactly sure what to do, but if someone can show me, I'd like to help." That voice was Grapecall's.

Ezra kneeled down and faced the young time traveler. "You're a courageous boy," the chief policeman told him. "One day, when you're older, I think your acts of bravery will help people around the world in ways you cannot yet imagine. But that day is not today." Ezra gave the boy a hug. "We'll find another way."

A loud crash shook the cave walls. Stones fell from the ceiling. Dust rose up from the floor.

"Our friend has found us," yelled Yoder. "The magic surrounding Agathon and Teodor must have lead him here."

Another crash followed by a roar. More debris rained down. It was getting difficult to see and breathe.

"He's trying to collapse the rock wall and bury us alive," Ezra shouted back.

And then a horrible shrieking noise erupted from within the cave as if a thousand dinosaurs bellowed in unison. A noise so deafening that hands shot up and covered every ear. Every ear except Fauntleroy's. For he was making the noise. "I told the dinosaur that we were coming out."

***

Fauntleroy stood hidden in shadow inside the entrance of the cave, his back pressed against the rocky wall. Sweat beaded across his forehead, ran down his back, and dampened the palms of his hands. Through the cave's opening he could see the tree trunk legs and clawed feet of the *Tyrannosaurus rex*. He could smell the beast's pungent odor. And he felt as if he could hear his own heart beating.

"Stall for time," Ezra had told Fauntleroy. "And whatever you do, do not leave the cave until I catch up with you." So Fauntleroy waited for the chief policeman just a few feet from what looked like certain doom.

"A voice. I thought I heard a voice," the *T. rex* roared, the nearness of his words making Fauntleroy tremble. "But the years have made me mad. So now the mountain must come down!"

"Wait," Fauntleroy shouted in dinosaur language from inside the cave. "You did hear a voice."

"You speak, but you do not show yourself. Were you sent by the wizard?"

Wizard? What was that giant lizard talking about? And where was Ezra?

"I do not know this wizard you speak of for I am not of your time. Guarantee my safety and I will walk into the light."

"I am Kahlee. On my honor as one of the Nazeen, if you come out you will not be harmed." And then the *T. rex* made a sound Fauntleroy could not recognize. Was the dinosaur laughing?

As Fauntleroy was deciding whether he preferred being eaten by the dinosaur or waiting for the creature to smash the mountain, Ezra appeared dragging a huge jagged rock that was almost as tall as Fauntleroy himself. He passed the rock to Fauntleroy and after a few quick whispers, receded into the dark cavern. Fauntleroy, rock in hand, went out to meet his fate.

"You meet with a weapon, but I am not afraid," roared the creature. "Throw your rock if you must!"

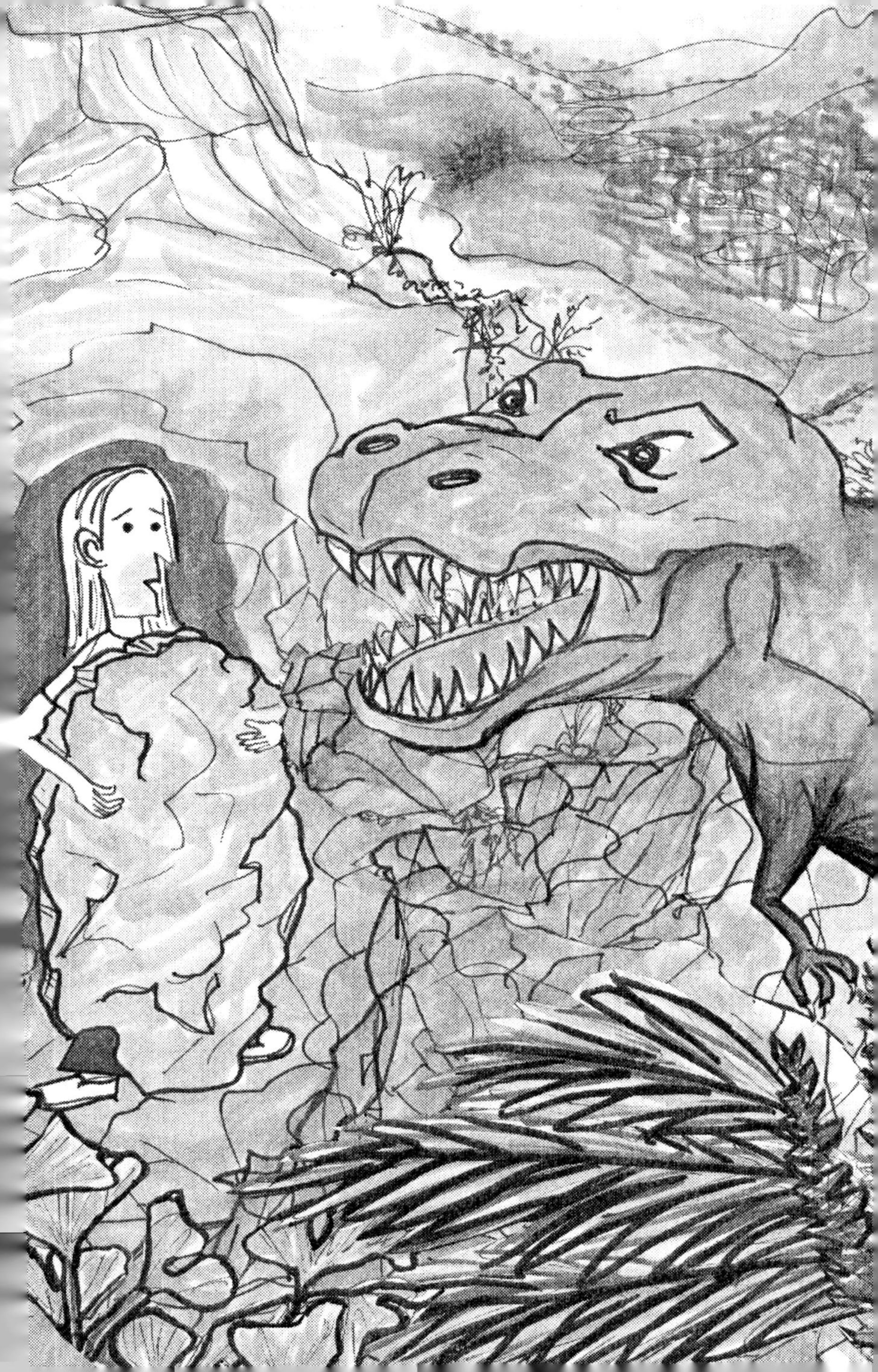

"I will only throw it if I need to," Fauntleroy roared back. "If you value your life, release my friends from your magic." Fauntleroy looked into the eyes of the *T. rex* and his teeth started to chatter.

The *T. rex* could smell Fauntleroy's fear. "Your friends belong to me now. Oh how the wizard would cry if he only knew how I have kept myself alive all these decades while imprisoned in this crude form. Yes, he used my own magic to transform me into this vile creature before you. But little did he know I could still use the energy to transform other creatures. And feast on their life forces. I will not release your friends. They will remain as they are until I have eaten all their energy and they fade into nothingness."

Fauntleroy's arms ached from the weight of the rock. He longed to put it down, but instead tightened his grip on it.

"You speak Nazareen well. I had forgotten what it was like to talk like civilized men," continued the *T. rex*. "For this I thank you. But I hunger. It is time for you to join your friends. I think you will make a fine caterpillar!"

The Tyrannosaurus's eyes glowed red, two ruby colored beams shooting straight for the policeman of many languages. With his very last ounce of energy Fauntleroy turned the rock around revealing the mirror-like surface from the cave wall. The beams reflected off the rock and back towards the creature hitting him in the arm and chest. The *T. rex* shrieked in agony. Its head whipped back and forth, eye beams blasting trees, mountain, and earth as it ran off into the forest.

Fauntleroy dropped the rock and sat down on it. Ezra, who had watched from the cave, ran out to him.

"You okay?" asked Ezra.

For the first time in his life Fauntleroy was speechless.

* * *

As Fauntleroy and Ezra returned to the cave of the old man a remarkable transformation was taking place. The puny tortoise and the glowworm were getting bigger and bigger. Growing legs and arms. Necks and human heads. Until before them stood Agathon and Teodor. Ezra's plan had worked. After the *T. rex* had injured itself, it no longer had the energy to block the magic of the Plape Leaves.

"My best hook!" Agathon cried out in disbelief, running over to his climbing tool now bent and battered. As he picked it up he noticed the cave wall was missing a huge chunk of rock roughly as tall as Fauntleroy. "Grappling hook for climbing rock. Not for digging rock!"

Ezra, Fauntleroy, Bjarne, Yoder, Frumbles and Grapecall enjoyed a good laugh (as did Agathon and Teodor once they learned why the grappling hook had ended up in such a poor state). Everyone was happy. They were all together and alive. Then carousel lights flooded the cave and everyone was even happier. The troublesome time machine had returned. Home was just a few million years away.

15

Ezra

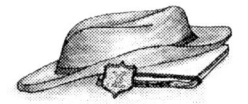

For the briefest moment, seven policemen and one Grapecall stood watching The Man's invention come into focus, a ghost-like image achieving solid form. And then Ezra's voice shattered the moment.

"Everyone, quick, inside the time machine!"

Grabbing Grapecall, Ezra ran with the boy in his arms into the small room that had just materialized. Teodor, Bjarne, Fauntleroy, and Yoder quickly followed realizing that they couldn't risk having the time machine leave without them again. And Agathon close on their heels pushed and shoved, squeezing his massive frame into the machine as well.

However when Frumbles reached The Man's invention, the entrance was blocked by what can only be described as a huge blob of smushed policeman. Almost every inch of the machine's inside space was filled. And no matter how hard the policemen tried to shift their bodies, no matter how hard Frumbles tried to wedge himself inside the doorway, there was no room for an additional passenger.

The officers exited and entered again and again, each time choosing a different policeman to be the last one to try to squeeze into the time machine. But regardless of who was chosen to enter last, there was never enough space to fit that final policeman.

Six disheartened policemen began to exit the time machine yet again, but just as Bjarne was separating his ear from Yoder's elbow a loud bell reverberated throughout the cabin. Everyone turned towards the sound. Mounted on the wall of The Man's invention was the Time Phone. And it was ringing.

"Hello?"

"Ezra, is that you? This is The Man. Please please tell me you've found Grapecall. We're almost out of time!"

* * *

Ezra slumped to the ground, his head in his hands. The Man had explained that he no longer trusted the time machine to work properly. That the more time his invention spent in the past, the less likely he would be able to control its journey back to the present. If the policemen and Grapecall didn't return within the next eight minutes, they might never make their way home again.

"So one of us stays in the past a bit longer," Frumbles suggested. "And then, after dropping off the others, the time machine comes back and picks him up, right?"

"The Man said that time was always moving, both in the future and the past. He said he wouldn't be able to calculate where to send the time machine a second time. That he only found us again because he had someone helping him." Ezra took a deep breath. "One of us will have to remain here."

Almost instantaneously, as if all six of

the remaining policeman and the one true Grapecall were of one mind, a chorus of voices said "I'll stay" in unison. Ezra looked at each of their faces, every man and boy before him willing to give up his life for the sake of the others. He smiled.

"It has been my great good honor to serve with all of you," the chief policeman told them. Then Ezra removed his badge from where it hung on his belt and handed it to Grapecall. "I'd like you to have this." Grapecall tried to say thank you, but the words stuck in his throat.

And that was that. The chief policemen had made his decision. Each policeman solemnly shook Ezra's hand before returning to the time machine. Grapecall, the tears running down his cheeks, hugged Ezra as hard as he could and would not let go until Bjarne gently pulled him away. Yoder took one last look at his colleague standing alone in the cave and then closed the time machine's door. He said something into the Time Phone and then disappeared.

* * *

It was as if Ezra had a hole in the pit of his stomach that was gouged out by a crazed hamster who was drinking lemonade and occasionally spitting the sour stuff out of his mouth. Ezra imagined the lemonade was causing the inside of his tummy to sizzle and burn, but he knew full well that his discomfort was being caused by a terrible feeling that something was not right. And an even more terrible feeling that if he could just figure out what was wrong, he might be able to find a way to escape from being trapped 80 million years in the past.

Images and words filled Ezra's thoughts.

The time machine, the *T. rex*, Plape Leaves, Frumbles amazing archery skills, the Time Phone, and The Man. Yes, The Man. He had said something in that last phone conversation. What was it?

And then it was there. That thing that Ezra had missed. It all made sense now. All he had to do was test his theory. And that could only be done at one location.

Ezra ran as fast as he could through the long passageway that lead back to the cave's entrance. Cool air hit his face and the only sound to be heard were the crickets outside and the faint snoring of the porcupine hedgehog that slept against the wall a few feet away.

"You know, I really don't believe in coincidences," Ezra said in a loud voice. "How is it that the time machine returned to us just when we needed it most? The Man told me someone had helped him figure out how to send it back to us. I find it odd that someone would just appear at his doorstep in the nick of time to help him."

"And why does it seem like some unknown person has also been helping me and the other policemen? It's very strange that just when we had no way to find Grapecall, the Time Phone was replaced with a brick that told us to go to the cave of the old man."

"But what bothers me most of all," and now Ezra was speaking directly to the porcupine hedgehog, "is that you and I have met before. You were in the cave when we visited the 96-year-old Grapecall. How is it that I've seen you twice—once now and once 87 years in the future—but you look exactly the same both times?" The creature stirred, opening its eyes. It stared motionlessly at Ezra.

"Only one answer is possible. You are not who you appear to be. You are the chess master, pushing seven policemen and a single Grapecall through time as if we were pawns on your cosmic chess board."

A rush of wind, a whirring sound, and a loud pop. The porcupine hedgehog had turned into a man dressed in flowing robes.

16

The Chess Master

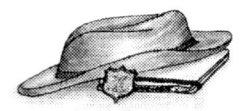

Ezra felt his heart beating inside his chest. *There is nothing to fear here,* he told himself. But knowing and believing are two different things, and Ezra did not quite believe what he knew to be true. The chief policeman took a deep breath and extended his hand.

"Hello. I'm Ezra."

"I know," the robed man answered. "It's been a long time since I last saw you. Much much longer than it's been since you saw me." He smiled as they shook hands.

Among his other talents, Ezra was a pretty good judge of character. He was relatively certain that the robed man wasn't lying to him. But if he wasn't lying, what exactly was he saying?

"You do look familiar," Ezra admitted, "but I'm sorry. I don't think we've ever met."

The robed figure stroked his beard, his smile fading slightly as if he were having second thoughts about what was to come. Then he pulled back a section of his robe to reveal something old and tarnished attached to his belt. It was a 7 Policemen badge.

"That badge...." Ezra didn't want to believe what he was thinking.

"You gave it to me when I was nine years old."

"Grapecall?"

"A little taller and a lot older, but yes, it's me," the robed figure acknowledged.

If this is Grapecall as an adult, it means that he is from my future, Ezra thought. *This is the Grapecall that I will know if I live to be a very old man.* But out loud, all Ezra could think to say was "How?"

Grapecall sat down on the floor of the cave and sighed deeply. "When I was nine I was accidentally transported back through the centuries in my father's time machine and was stranded in the prehistoric era. My father asked The 7 Policemen to rescue me."

"I know this," Ezra interrupted.

"No, you don't," Grapecall countered. "You and the other policemen traveled 80 million years into the past and found me waiting for you. Four policemen took me back to my father and then the time machine returned for the three who stayed behind. You never met the *T. rex*. You never went to the cave of the Old Man. Bringing me home went smoothly and was over in just a few hours. And you don't remember any of this because that was *the first time you rescued me*."

Ezra decided to sit down as well.

"I grew up, earned several college degrees, and became a scientist. I improved on my father's invention, making it extremely reliable and small enough to fit in the palm of my hand." Grapecall opened his fist to reveal a device that looked like a tube with a button on top and several others around its circumference. "I traveled throughout history, witnessing ancient cultures and learning about humanity. Then, on a trip to the prehistoric era, I encountered an alien from a far off galaxy. He attacked me, red beams of light shooting out of his eyes. I dove behind a crystalline rock. The eye beams reflected off the rock, hit the alien, and turned it into the *T. rex*."

Ezra needed to interrupt. "Are you saying that there was a different version of history where Grapecall—who is you—grows up to become a time traveler? But this adult Grapecall—again YOU—changes his own past?"

"Yes," Grapecall continued. "Time had shifted. Nine-year-old me had no longer been saved by The 7 Policemen. I would grow up in the time of the caveman. I would remain lost in the past and destined to live out my life in this cave."

"But shouldn't you have disappeared as soon as history changed?" Ezra asked. "I mean, if your life was spent in a cave, you never became a scientist. You never refined the time machine. You never grew up to become time traveling Grapecall."

"My time machine protected me. It emits an energy field that surrounds my body while

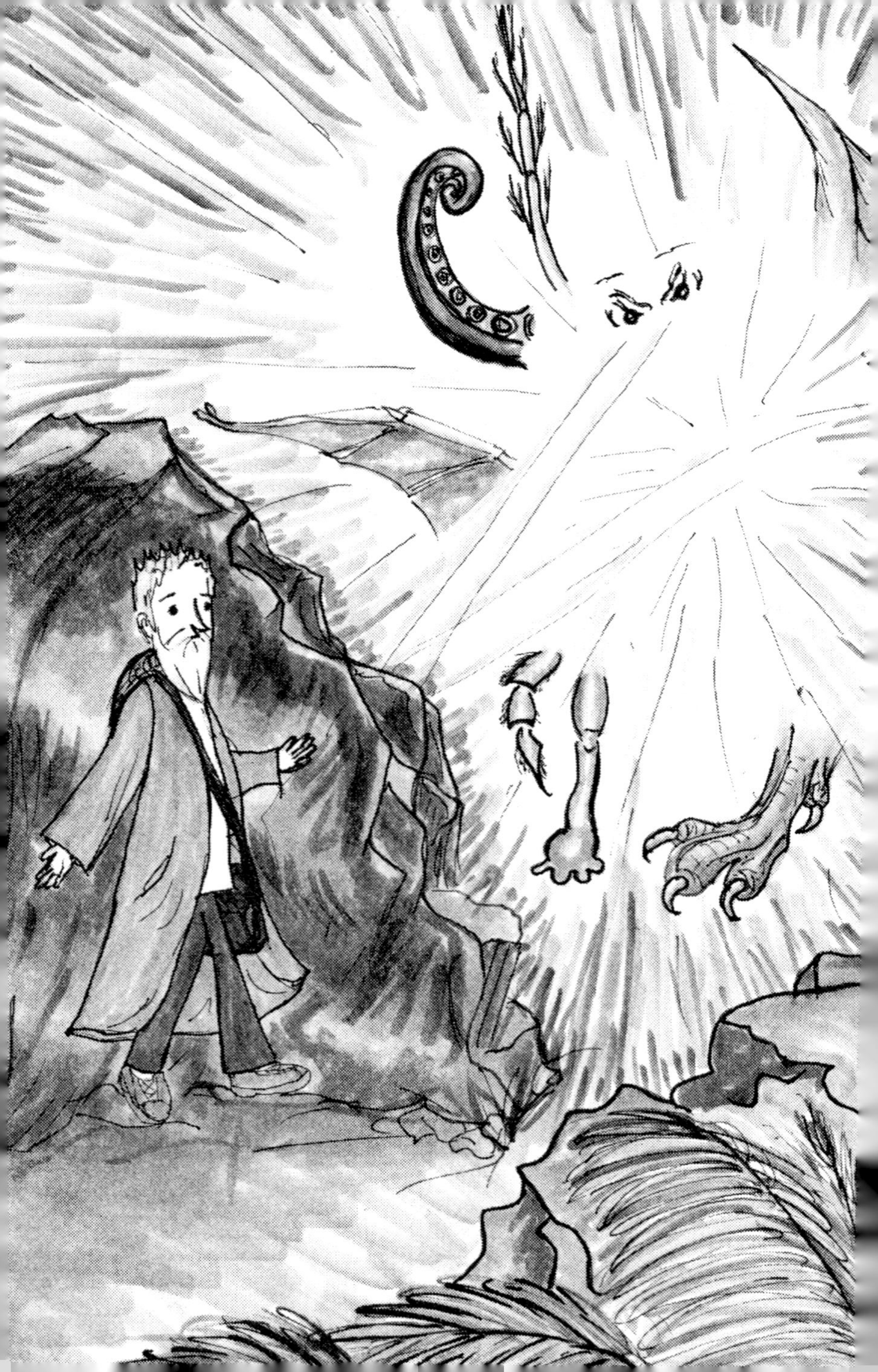

I travel in time. This field keeps me in a state that's slightly 'outside of the current time,' so that when time changes around me, as it does frequently and naturally, I am not affected," Grapecall explained. "But should the batteries that power my time machine run out of energy, I would no longer be protected, and I would cease to exist. So I had to try to repair time before that could happen. Or as you stated earlier, I had to become the chess master."

"You made all of this happen." Ezra rubbed his eyes while trying to make sense of what Grapecall had told him. "When we first went back in time it was you who stopped the Time Phone from working."

"I blocked the signal so my father wouldn't interfere with my plan."

"And let me guess, you tricked the *T. rex* into attacking us the first time."

"I didn't want to." Grapecall sighed. "But I needed a way to get you all back into your time machine at that precise moment. I then used my handheld time machine to help you travel further back in time to meet me as an old man."

"You also guided us to this time we're in right now."

"Teodor did most of the hard work to get you here," Grapecall said, "but yes, after you used the tally marks to figure out where my nine-year-old self was, I made sure you arrived exactly when I needed you to."

The two men sat in silence. Ezra absentmindedly drew circles with his foot in the dirt on the cave floor. Grapecall waited for the question he knew would come, but which he was ashamed to answer. He didn't have to wait long.

"How could you possibly have predicted that Frumbles would turn into an expert archer," asked Ezra. "That he would save us from the *T. rex* after Agathon and Teodor were transformed into a glowworm and tortoise?"

"I didn't," answered Grapecall. "Not at first. I'm so sorry." Grapecall looked down at his hands. "Frumbles was never supposed to be one of The 7 Policemen. Before I changed history, there was another person in your group instead of Frumbles. But without Frumbles, the *T. rex* defeats

The 7 Policemen."

"Another policeman?" Ezra was not sure he wanted to hear anymore.

"I knew that the only way I could repair history was to have The 7 Policemen defeat the *T. rex*," continued Grapecall. "But the original 7 Policemen couldn't do it. So I traveled back to the point in time when there were only six policemen in your group and I convinced you to hire Frumbles. By doing so I erased a large part of the original history of The 7 Policemen. A history that had someone other than Frumbles accompany you on your cases. This is also the reason most people cannot remember Frumbles. Somehow their brains sense something is wrong and cannot accept that he is a member of your group."

"We don't remember any of this because when pieces of history were erased, so were our memories of those events," Ezra reasoned.

"Please know that I am so so sorry."

Ezra's head hurt. He couldn't imagine The 7 Policemen without Frumbles. History being changed by a time traveler from the future? Not remembering things that had happened because they were now erased? All true, but there was nothing he could do now except continue on. In this time. Where he was now.

"You knew Frumbles was born with incredible archery skills," said Ezra, "because you had traveled to a future when Frumbles was older. To the time he would eventually discover his talent for using a bow and arrow. But you changed that history too. Now Frumbles discovers his talent for archery just in time to save us from the *T. rex.*"

"Yes."

"But I remember the day Frumbles joined The 7 Policemen quite clearly. It was Yoder who recommended Frumbles." A rush of wind, a whirring sound, and a loud pop. Right before Ezra's eyes, Grapecall turned into Yoder.

"My handheld time machine gives me the ability to take a picture of any living thing at any point in history," Grapecall revealed. "I can surround myself with that image, appearing as anyone I choose. And I assure you, it was I who convinced you to ask Frumbles to join the group. Just as I assure you that later that same day, I impersonated you and convinced the other policemen that it was your idea to have Frumbles become the 7th policeman."

The two men stood up and Grapecall became Grapecall again. "It is time for you to return to your own time," Grapecall said. "But when we see my father, you cannot reveal to him or to my younger self that I am future Grapecall. If they had this knowledge, it would change history again. I might not grow up to be who I am now. I might not be able to help you as I have done these past few days."

Ezra understood. If nothing else, Grapecall's story had taught him how fragile time was. How one change in history, no matter how small, could alter the course of future events. Ezra would not allow that to happen again.

17

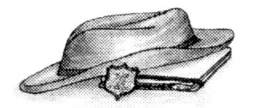

Egmont

As Ezra materialized in The Man's living room he could see the inventor and his son, now reunited, with their arms tightly around each other. Six heavy-hearted policemen stood off to the side watching them, quietly happy for Grapecall and his father, yet sad for having left their leader back in the past. But upon seeing Ezra, everyone ran to hug the chief policeman, whoops of joy replacing the quiet reunion of moments before. However, smiles turned into questions when the group gazed upon future Grapecall.

"He's a friend," Ezra announced to the room, not wanting to say too much for fear of changing the future. "He helped me get back here."

Ezra didn't know what else to say. Tell the truth and the past and future might change. Say nothing, and the other policemen would not stop until they solved the mystery of the robed man's identity. But then Fauntleroy showed Ezra the solution.

"Are you the wizard the *T. rex* spoke about," Fauntleroy asked.

"Yes," answered future Grapecall. "I am Egmont. Sworn enemy of the *T. rex*."

Yoder leaned his head slightly towards Ezra's, and as quietly as possible whispered, "He's lying." Ezra's body jerked slightly. "Egmont claims to be a wizard, but it's not possible," continued Yoder. "He does not have a magical aura."

Ezra nodded. *One day Yoder will figure out that Egmont is really adult Grapecall from the future*, thought Ezra. *It's only a matter of time.*

Ezra felt a tugging at his sleeve. It was nine-year-old Grapecall, an outstretched hand returning the chief policeman's badge.

"It's yours," the smiling boy told him. "You

should take it back."

But as Ezra glanced back at future Grapecall he caught a glimpse of his old tarnished badge pinned to the time traveler's belt.

"No, you should keep it," Ezra replied. "It's my gift to you. I have a feeling it will come in handy one day when you're much older."

The air inside The Man's house suddenly grew colder and lightning bolts rang out of a clear sky.

"He has come," shouted future Grapecall. "Prepare yourselves!" The fake wizard raised both his arms to the sky, one hand frantically pushing buttons on the time travel device strapped to its palm. The Man's house and all it contained—every sticky wall, every stained possession—vanished.

The 7 Policemen, the two Grapecalls, and The Man stood on the plot of land where the house rested moments ago, drenching rain hurtling out of the now dark and treacherous clouds above them. Two giant scaly feet landed like an earthquake on the ground before them followed by an all too familiar roar.

But the *T. rex* was roaring in pain. One arm had been transformed into a frog leg and the beast's chest was now black and bumpy as if the ray that had hit him there had changed his reptile skin into the black casing of a beetle.

Future Grapecall raised his arms skyward again and The 7 Policemen, Grapecall, and The Man found themselves dressed in full armor and chainmail, swords ready in their scabbards except for Frumbles, who had a bow with a full quiver slung across his shoulder. The fake wizard, also in armor, wielded a mace, its' spiked metal ball flying in a circle above his raised arm.

"He won't shoot his eye beams at you," the fake wizard shouted. "Your armor is reflective and the beams will just bounce off. Attack!"

Frumbles was first to respond shooting arrow after arrow into the giant reptile's neck. Fauntleroy, Bjarne, and Teodor charged the

T. rex from behind. Yoder and Agathon struck from either side. And Ezra faced the monster head-on, swinging his sword at the creature's lunging jaws.

But then the unthinkable happened. Like some gruesome prehistoric ballet dancer, the *T. rex* spun around, its tail striking everything in its way. And in its way were Yoder, Fauntleroy, Bjarne, Teodor, Agathon and Frumbles. Six policemen flying through the air, armor crashing into the hard ground.

Then with its one good arm the lizard knocked Ezra to the ground sending the police chief's sword skittering. Ezra, crawling on his back, tried to get away from the creature as it roared in triumph inches from the policeman's face. The lizard's breath smelled like rotting meat mixed with tar and dung. The creature reared back, opened its jaws and lunged for Ezra's head. Only a second now and it would all be over. The jaws closed and the teeth sunk into metal. But not the metal of Ezra's armor. Future Grapecall had swung his mace into the creature's open mouth, the pain forcing the dinosaur to jerk back and miss Ezra's head by inches.

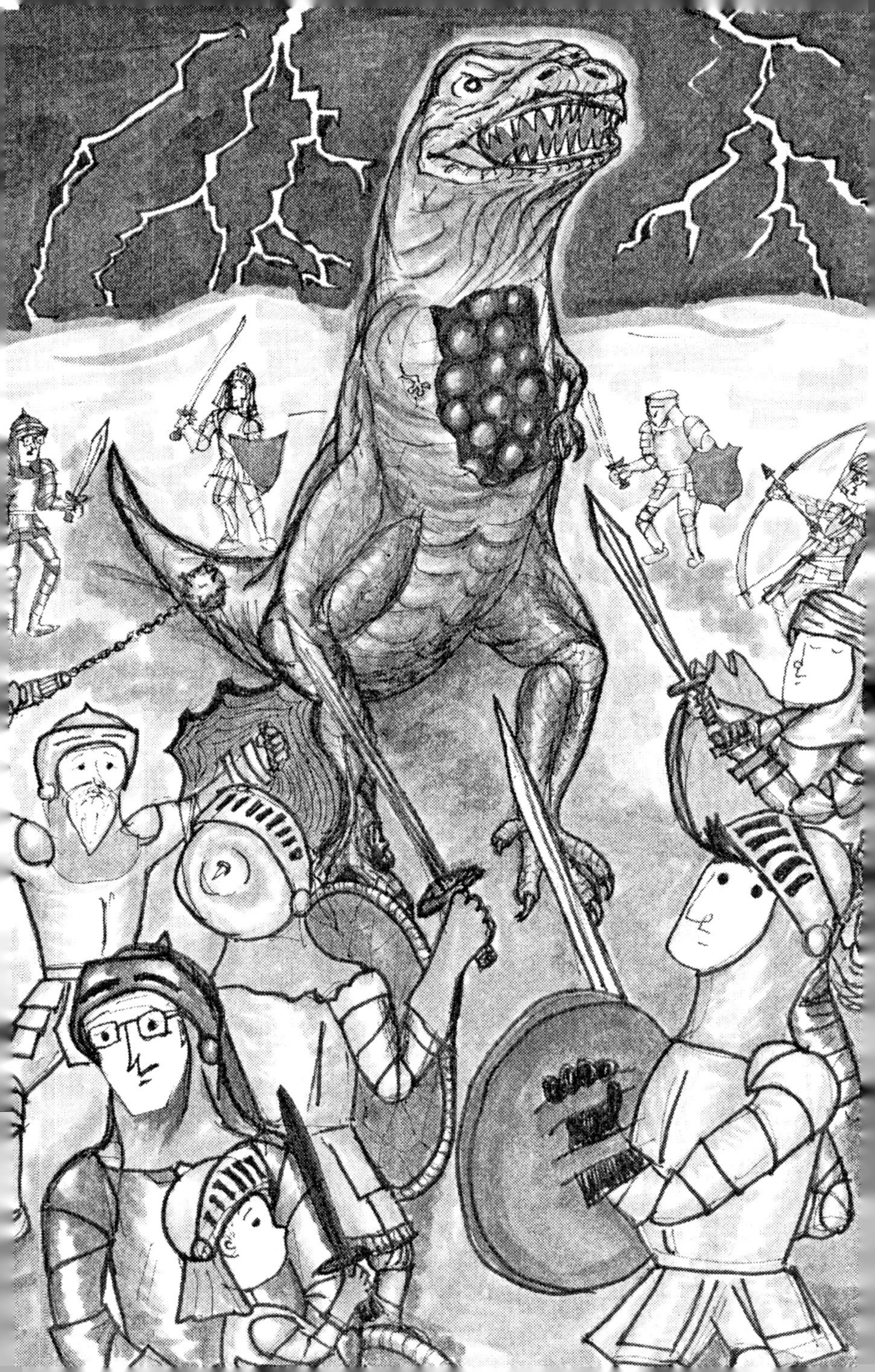

The monster stood up to its full height and the fake wizard, still holding the handle of his mace, dangled from the creature's mouth. Before Rex could shake his head back and forth in an attempt to dislodge the mace and its owner, future Grapecall raised his free arm, swirling lights shooting out of his fist. The lights formed themselves into rings encircling both monster and time traveler and creating a fifteen foot tall cocoon that buzzed and hummed. In a flash of light they were gone. In another flash The Man's house returned. And on the final burst of light the armor and weapons disappeared.

Ezra looked around. The other policeman, though battered and bruised, had been saved by their armor. The Man and Grapecall were together again. And despite the puddles their soaking wet bodies were leaving on the floor, The Man's house was basically undamaged.

"I'm hungry," Grapecall announced. Everything finally seemed back to normal.

* * *

After drying themselves off in front of the fireplace, The 7 Policemen, Grapecall, and

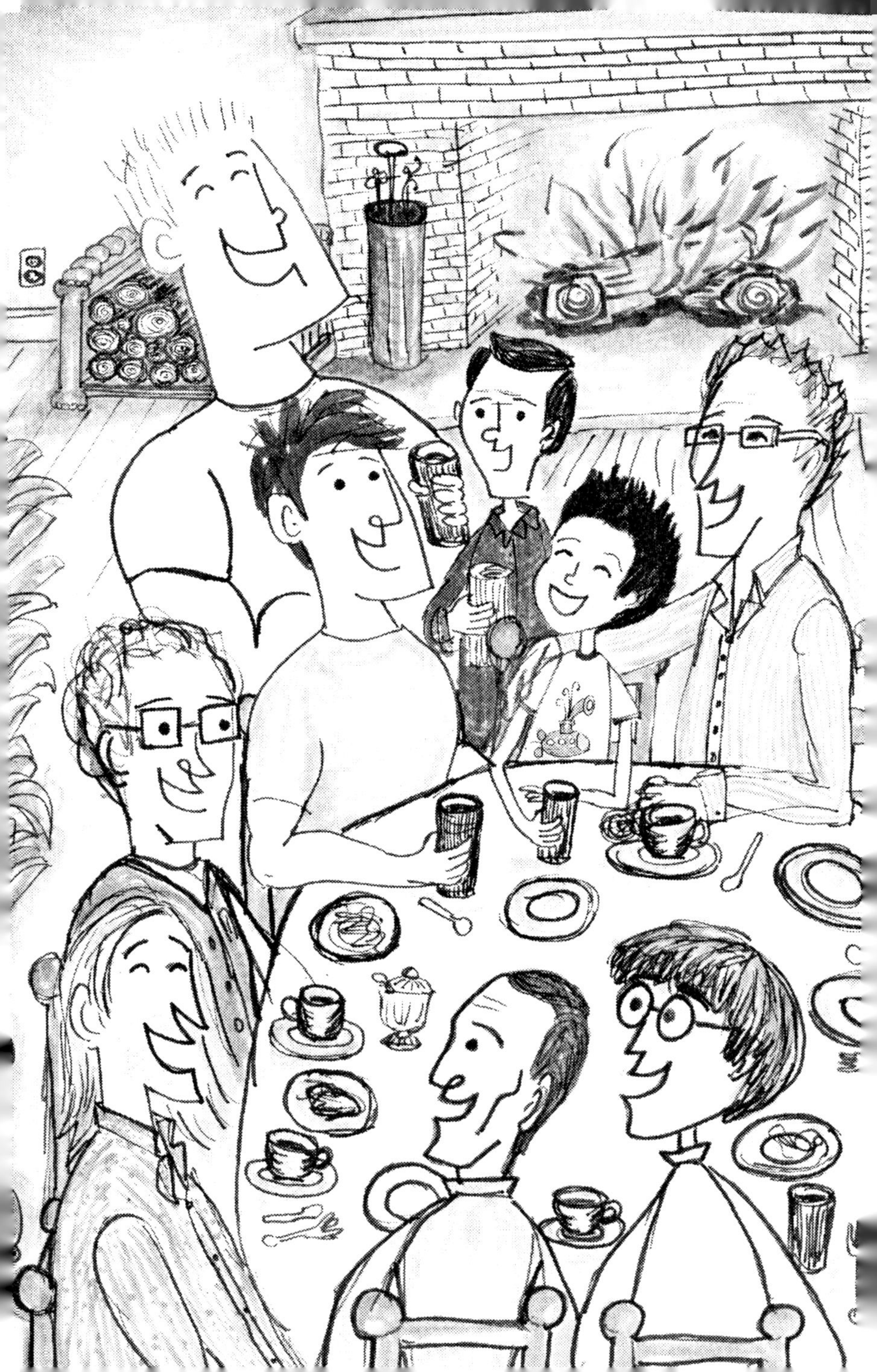

The Man sat down to a well-deserved dinner. Everyone shared their part in the adventure. The policemen recounted how they found Grapecall. The Man spoke of how Egmont helped him send the time machine back to the policemen and his son. And Grapecall described what it was like living in the prehistoric past for three weeks.

But Ezra did not say a word. He did not reveal that Egmont was really future Grapecall. That future Grapecall pretended to be a wizard, but actually had used his handheld time machine to save The Man's house from being destroyed by the *T. rex*. That future Grapecall had used that same machine to bring armor from the past to protect everyone from an alien that had been transformed into a dinosaur. No, Ezra remained silent. He just listened to everyone's stories and smiled.

As the policemen were leaving The Man's house, Ezra turned to the time machine's inventor and shook his hand. "If you ever need The 7 Policemen again, you know how to reach us."

The Man wrapped his arms around

Ezra and embraced him. "Thank you for everything."

Ezra pulled the knob and closed the door behind him as he left The Man's house. Grapecall had been returned to his father. The 7 Policemen were back in the present. But one last thing left Ezra feeling a bit uncomfortable. It was the palm of his hand. It was covered in peanut butter.

Epilogue

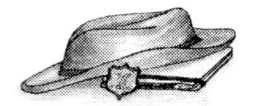

Later that evening, back at the headquarters of The 7 Policemen, not one of the officers could sleep. Agathon was up half the night devising plans for a worm farm. Teodor felt an uncontrollable urge to learn as much as humanly possible about the lives of tortoises. Frumbles set up an archery range in back of the building, practicing until dawn. Bjarne gazed into his microscope for hours studying plant samples he brought back from 80 million years ago. And Fauntleroy began jotting down notes for what would become a Dinosaur-English dictionary.

Yoder was the only one of the policemen who tried to go to sleep, but he couldn't set his mind at ease. *Why did Egmont call himself a wizard, when there was nothing magical about him? And if he had no magic, how did he do all those incredible feats?* Yoder felt he couldn't rest until he got some answers.

While Yoder tossed and turned in his bed, Ezra paced the floor of his own room. Future Grapecall had said that Frumbles was not originally a member of The 7 Policemen. That before history had been changed, another had been in his place. Who was that policeman? It didn't seem right that someone's entire life could be changed because of a time traveler's mistake. Ezra wanted to set things right, but how?

Unlike The 7 Policemen, The Man and nine-year-old Grapecall had no trouble sleeping that night. As soon as the officers left their home, the happy yet exhausted pair went straight to bed and within seconds fell into a deep deep sleep. So deep that they never heard the very loud ringing coming from the time machine. Or more exactly from the Time Phone. Which rang 16 times. And then stopped.

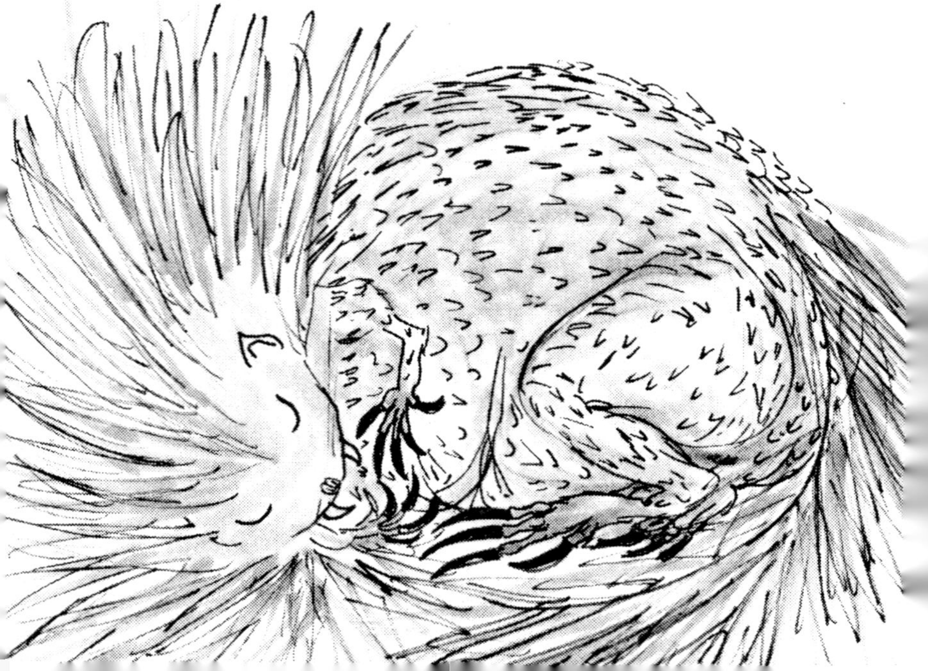